STONES AND
SHADOWS

Jane Nancarrow

TO THE MEMORY OF MY DEAR AUNT
RUTH MARY HOBBS

PUBLISHED BY SCRYFA

WWW.SCRYFA.CO.UK

DESIGNED AND EDITED BY SIMON PARKER

COVER PHOTOGRAPH: GARROW BY JULIA CHALMERS

FIRST PUBLISHED BY SCRYFA 2010

REPRINTED BY SCRYFA 2012

ISBN 978-0-9563990-1-4

PRINTED BY SRP

THE young man's tousled hair was wet, either with sweat or water. His lifeless body flopped, like a rag doll. His neck was broken, surely. 'What a drop that was,' murmured an official, wearing some kind of uniform, as he looked down on the corpse.

'They d'say he had been very depressed over the past few weeks,' croaked the voice of a much older man among the bystanders.

'Wouldn't you have been?'

A bitter tone from a much younger voice was the response.

'This place is enough to depress anyone.'

They rolled the man's body over on to his back. Sightless eyes stared up at the onlookers through the tangle of dark wet curls. A whisper could be heard in the awful silence.

'Couldn't it all have been a tragic accident?'

The man in uniform shook his head.

'Whichever way you look at it, the young man's dead. Waste of a young life, I'd say.'

'You mean it's a tragedy for the girl, don't you? His lover? The one who lived in the farmhouse with him?'

'They say he was out of his mind. And she must have been blind not to see it coming.'

The first man shook his head again.

'Too wrapped up in herself to see what was happening, by all accounts.'

'Which one of these two lovers deserves our prayers the most, I wonder?'

They all turned to see the man in black who had spoken these quiet words.

'We must reap what we sow in this life. And pray for mercy in the next.'

ONE

POPPY stood at the door to the grey cottage facing the solemn tors, the wind whipping her wild red hair. Pre-Raphaelite, Matt had called it. She'd liked that. A strand of hair caught in her mouth and she brushed it away. She ran her fingers over the granite lintel. It felt rough, warm, in the early spring sunshine. She took a deep breath and pushed the heavy wooden door open. It grated on the slate slabs. The remote cottage at Penhale was built of weathered granite, its deep-set windows seemed small dark holes from the outside.

'Too dark for an artist,' thought Poppy. 'Too lonely and bare for a woman seeking some kind of escape. And yet… there is a good atmosphere here somehow. At one with nature.'

She walked across the slabs towards the window, her footsteps echoing as if in a vault. She gazed out at the distant tors. The small garden, or yard, was of rough grass and scrub. It was littered with the droppings of sheep and cattle, enclosed by a mossy dry-stone wall. The remains of a derelict outhouse stood by the gate. Gnarled, twisted trees clawed at the slated roof of the cottage. Everything was of slate or granite in this brooding moorland kingdom, she mused.

'You can't seriously be thinking of living out here?'

A voice broke into her reverie. A warm Cornish voice. The daylight was blocked from the open doorway by the broad shoulders and muscular body of a young man, stooping as he hovered on the threshold of the ancient cottage.

'It's too isolated for one thing.'

She turned to look at her friend, Josh. For once, his honest comments riled her.

'Why shouldn't I live here? It's perfect. I want to get away from the world, remember?'

He could see the pain etched in her face, her green eyes brimming with the tears that were never far away these days.

'Come on Poppy, be realistic. It's a bloody hovel!' Josh gave a derisive snort.

'My father said no one's lived out here for ages.'

She turned again to the window and its view of the open moorland, with wild horses grazing the rough grass. Could she live out here without Matt? In fact, she thought, could she live anywhere without Matt? She was still unable to believe he was gone. The finality refused to sink in to her confused state of mind.

'It was an old shepherd's cottage, Father said. Old Tom Sandercock was probably the last person he knew to actually live out here, but he was used to remote places. Always been a shepherd, always lived on his own, so he didn't know any different.'

She was quiet, immersed in her own thoughts. Josh persisted.

'Wise up a bit, Poppy. You'd be here on your own most of the time, miles from anywhere.'

He paused.

'Unless you think some dark, handsome bloke like that Heathcliff you're always on about will suddenly appear out of the mist at the garden gate. Life's not really like your beloved novels when it comes down to it.'

She gave him the faintest of smiles and pointed towards the narrow staircase.

'Let's have a look upstairs, you may change your mind.'

Josh creaked up the wooden stairs heavily behind her, with a leaden heart. He knew how wayward Poppy could be when she had an idea fixed in her mind.

'Oh it's really lovely!' she said passionately. 'Look at this quaint little window seat.'

She wiped some dirt off the tiny window-pane with the cuff of her old coat and peered out.

'What an amazing view, Josh. I can just imagine sitting here with a book, and the sun shining in.'

'And what about all those days when it's pouring with bloody rain and you can't see a thing out of the window but sodding sheep?'

'But you know me, I like anything with a bit of character.'

She smiled at him with her startling green eyes. Why was she so extraordinarily beautiful? All he knew was that he felt drawn to this woman, his close friend from schooldays, no matter what she did. He would try much harder to be flippant with her.

'To use one of my Gran's old sayings, "you're as maze as a brush" for even thinking of living out here. You're miles from the nearest hamlet.'

Josh stopped as a sudden thought occurred to him.

'And you'd need a generator for one thing, living this far out on the moor.'

Poppy pushed past him impatiently and clattered down the stairs. Her pale face was flushed and she had a determined expression as she went out and stood in the patch of wild garden. She was frowning into the distance, stubbornly chewing her reddening lips, when Josh emerged from the dark interior.

'I mean it Poppy, you'd have to have a "jenny" for your power if you did live out here. It would be a right bloody pain.'

His kind eyes were troubled and full of real concern.

He knew only too well that she showed all the signs of becoming hooked on this crazy idea.

'But I like the feel of the cottage. There is a friendly aura. It seems like I have come home in some strange way.'

She swept her eyes over the wild landscape. Was that a gleam of silvery water she could discern in the distance?

'I might even be inspired to paint again, surrounded by all this rugged beauty.'

There was a peaceful silence broken only by the sighing of the wind. He watched her far-off expression as he leaned against the doorway. And then she struck.

'I'm going to take it!'

Josh's chest tightened and he thought he could hear his heart groan loudly. He felt a hopeless resignation sweep over him.

'It's only a peppercorn rent anyway,' she said. 'It's perfect.'

And against all Josh's reasoned arguments, she had taken the cottage, signing an agreement for six months or more with a sharp-suited estate agent. Even he made it obvious he thought she must be mad. A frenzy of activity quickly followed. Josh and his father had worked hard on the outhouse, making it weather-proof once more. A generator was installed in one corner, where it nestled in the dirt and cobwebs between an ancient mangle and an old chest-of-drawers. Josh's father, who farmed at St Clether, was useful with mechanical problems of any sort and soon got the generator in working order. But he, too, made it quite clear that he thought Poppy must be completely barmy to want to live in such a remote place.

'I wouldn't want a daughter of mine to live out here on her own,' he'd said, taking off his inevitable farmer's cap and scratching his greying head as he surveyed the scene. 'It's enough to send you round the twist, all this emptiness. Why on earth don't you get a nice little place back home in Launceston? Or even Camelford, come to that?'

He shook his head once more and drove off in a battered Land-Rover, his faithful sheep-dog looking out the back, her ears ruffling in the wind. He would soon be regaling his wife with tales of Josh's crazy friend Poppy, no doubt. Josh helped her white-wash the interior walls of the tiny cottage and she had scrubbed the filthy slate slabs until she was exhausted. Brightly-coloured rugs were thrown on the floor and before long a fire flickered in the huge open fireplace. A dark shadowy corner revealed a cloam oven. A bowl of vivid blue hyacinths sat on the window-sill, their perfume heavy in the rays of sunlight. Some of Poppy's own paintings adorned the walls with their bright daubs of colour. A beautiful little oil painting of ducks at Lamorna, painted by Charles Simpson, was hung over the bookcase. It had belonged to her aunt, bought years ago at Penzance for a few pounds. The old shepherd's cottage began to take on new life.

'I won't be alone you see,' she whispered, as she held a big black cat tightly in her arms. Winston had been Matt's cat really, but now he was hers. Winston was not at all impressed with the many changes he'd had to endure recently. He soon struggled out of Poppy's arms and jumped up to the window-sill where he watched her from his sunny spot next to the bowl of hyacinths. Disdainfully he turned to look out of the window.

The bedroom looked really cosy. Josh had used all his muscles to manoeuvre the antique brass bedstead and mattress up the narrow staircase. Now the bed was made up and it looked comfortable and inviting. Jesus, he thought guiltily, how he'd love to throw those bloody silly cushions off the bed and lie in there with Poppy in his arms. Instead, he sweated streams and swore loudly as he lugged her heavy chest-of-drawers into place. She persuaded Josh to drag the old mangle out into the garden and clean it off before he'd had to get back to work at the farm. Poppy sang as she put her washing through the mangle. She sang as she hung the washing out on the line, her clothes flapping in the wind, the sheets rippling and cracking like the sails on a yacht. In that there was a feeling of freedom and a sense of madness. Childhood memories of days sailing at Fowey with her father and his friends came back in an instant.

After the elation of her spirit, she took out her paints and brushes and looked them over. She had not used them since Matt had died. A stack of dusty-looking canvases stood in a corner of the room, which served as both kitchen and living room. Poppy pulled out her last portrait of Matt and looked at it critically. Wild black hair and remarkable dark eyes. But now she looked at those eyes again, they looked sad. Lost.

'The eyes are the windows of the soul,' she murmured. 'Why couldn't I see the sadness there?'

That night, her first night in the cottage, sleep did not come easily. She got out of bed and sat by the tiny window. Somewhere in the vast darkness of the moorland came the bark of a dog-fox answered by the scream of a vixen.

'I am really alone,' she thought. She looked up at the distant stars and gave a shiver. She felt desolate. Her dreams of Matt, when sleep eventually came, were troubled and confused. Her world was still unreal.

Two

SHE had met Matt one hot summer at St Ives. Poppy had been staying in the Digey with Rosa, her friend from art college days. Both were excited at the thought of staying in the old fisherman's cottage of Rosa's aunt for the whole month of August while she was away in Cyprus.

The friends both adored swimming in the sea and painting, so it was to be a relaxing time for them both. She had swum a long way out in the sea, much further than Rosa, in the wonderfully warm water. Turning, she had looked back at the busy beach with its brightly coloured umbrellas. She floated on her back, looking up at a butter-yellow sun. An amazing sense of freedom washed over her. Later she had swum slowly back, to find Rosa baking on her towel on the sand, glistening like an oiled sardine. Rosa, with her brown gypsy looks; Poppy felt it was embarrassing to lie next to her on the beach with her own milk-white skin.

'Victorian ladies would have loved your skin,' Rosa laughed.

They felt too lazy to paint at first. What was that frenzy that took hold of artists like Van Gogh, so that they did not stop to eat or drink even? But then Poppy had been dazed by the pure light at Porthmeor. She had taken out her sketch book and paints. Days passed in a hazy blue blur of sea and sky. Both girls lazed and swam, while boats sailed in and out of the harbour. Then for a few days Rosa went away to Penzance to meet up with some cousins she had not seen for years.

'I shall hate every minute of it. Blood is most definitely not thicker than water,' she moaned.

'I shall probably be back tonight' were her last words before she clambered into her car, which was splattered with seagull droppings and white with salt. Poppy relished the feeling of freedom from Rosa and her incessant chatter, although she felt guilty. She pushed her way through the crowded narrow streets anonymously and ended up by the lifeboat station. The sun was blazing hot. The aroma of pasties wafted from a nearby bakery and mixed with the smell of coconut oil. By the quay a guitar-player, in a faded blue cotton shirt and ripped jeans, was busking. He looked up as Poppy passed by. He had the most remarkable eyes. She felt his glance brush over her like the wings of a bird. When his gaze met hers a shiver ran through her body like an electric shock.

'Oh my God,' she thought.

They stood and stared at each other while the summer crowds jostled around them. Later, in the warm evening, they had walked on the cliff path. Walked and talked of everything. They had wandered down to the harbour again. They sat in a bar and drank cold beer and ate Cornish mussels. They laughed at some of the holidaymakers strolling past, the women with red sunburned backs and arms, squeezed into bright, flowery summer dresses. Their husbands following docilely in their wake. Younger couples trundled pushchairs full of tired children along the front in the summer dusk. Out of the window Poppy saw a small boat with green sails sailing across the bay, which looked just like one of Alfred Wallis's paintings. She felt she could burst with happiness that evening. It was the end of the day that she had met Matt. And it was the beginning of something special, something in the stars.

The sea was silver and brilliant in the moonlight when they eventually meandered up the narrow lanes to the Digey, hand in hand, Matt's guitar slung across his back. The tiny cottage was empty. Rosa had thankfully stayed in Penzance. Blood could well have proved thicker than water after all. In her simply-furnished white bedroom, Poppy slipped off her leather sandals. Her feet bare on sanded floorboards of wood. Matt pulled off his cotton shirt and held her and stroked her hair, long and tangled. She remembered the smell of the sea on Matt's sunkissed skin. The taste of salt on his lips. He unzipped his faded jeans and kicked them away. They lay, naked, in the summer night. Cool white sheets caressed them.

'Your hair is beautiful!'

He twisted a rope of her red hair around his fingers.

'Don't ever cut it... it's Pre- Raphaelite!'

She lay, shivering, in the warm night, as Matt made love to her. She remembered his mouth on her breasts, that first time. She remembered, too, the beautiful crucifix around his neck, silver against his olive skin.

The next morning they were awakened early by the gabble of gulls on the slate roof. They lay amidst rumpled bedclothes. She had been dazzled by the early sunlight... and Matt's wonderful eyes.

So started a magical summer for them both, delighting in each other's company. They had fallen in love that summer in St Ives. One perfect day they walked up to Zennor along the twisting road to St Just, past fields and huge granite boulders. Stone stacks and engine houses stood on the wild moorland. A lark high above them was trilling its timeless song. They visited the beautiful little parish church of St Senara, squat and grey. Inside in the musty, dim coolness they had stood by Zennor's famous mermaid, carved into a heavy oak pew, a comb in one hand and a looking-glass in the other.

'You are my beautiful mermaid,' Matt had whispered. 'You taste of the sea and your hair is like tendrils of seaweed.'

Again his mouth came down on hers, wet and salty... her heart thumping. She felt wet, soaking even...

Poppy woke, confused and wet with sour sweat. She was alone. Alone in an old shepherd's cottage. Not in Zennor in West Penwith, but out on Bodmin Moor. She felt disorientated, desolate. Once again she felt the pain of loneliness and the realisation that Matt was dead.

THREE

THE sun was high in the sky when Poppy made herself crawl out of bed. She had woken from a dream of past times. Now she had to face the nightmare of her loss all over again. She dragged on some crumpled clothes and looked at her face in the mirror. Pale. Exhausted. Mauve shadows under her dull eyes. Where was the beautiful mermaid now? Propped on the chest of drawers was her portrait of Matt. She had brought it upstairs with her the night before. It was the last thing she had seen before her troubled night's sleep. Now she sat on the end of the bed and just stared at it. She'd lost all sense of time, sitting there. If only she could reach out and touch his tousled black hair... see that generous mouth break into a smile. A sudden loud hammering on the outside door roused her from her stupor, made her tremble violently.

'Come on Poppy! Open up!'

Josh's deep voice carried distinctly up to the bedroom window from outside.

'Your supplies have arrived!'

Poppy's face lit up as she eagerly ran down the narrow stairs to unlock the door. As she lifted the heavy latch, Josh's weathered face was at the window where Winston had been sitting, washing himself. Now he gave Josh an insolent stare. Dear Josh. He was Poppy's closest friend. He had loved her, even when she shut him out under Matt's all-consuming spell. He lived near St Clether on the family farm where he and his father were converting some disused barns into holiday cottages.

'Here you are then: milk, coffee, crusty bread, good strong Davidstow cheddar and a couple of bottles of wine.'

Josh pushed through the open door, carrying a box.

'And my gran has made a pasty for your tea. "Can't have the maid starve" were her actual words.'

He ceremoniously dumped the box on the cluttered table. Poppy started to clear a space amongst the pile of books and papers. Josh's grin turned to a frown when he saw her face.

'You look bleddy awful!'

He turned to stare out of the window at the surrounding tors.

'I don't like it, you being out here on your own. It's too wild. Too isolated. It doesn't feel right leaving you out here, Poppy.'

Poppy pulled the cork and poured ruby-red liquid into two wine glasses. She passed one to Josh.

'I'm fine. It's what I need right now. Plenty of space and Cornish air.'

Poppy's voice tailed off, a slight tremor perceptible.

'I need to come to terms with my own company.'

Unusually, she ate ravenously, spreading butter on chunks of bread, with wedges of cheese. She washed it down with red wine that spoke of sunny far-off vineyards. Josh watched her over the rim of his glass.

'Bloody hell maid! Steady on with the plonk! You look as if you've only just got up. Did you have any breakfast?'

'Don't be such a pain, Josh. You sound just like my mother used to, when I was in my teens.'

Poppy's mother, Angie, had long since disappeared off the scene. After an acrimonious divorce from Poppy's father she had gone looking for pastures new, preferably with a rich man to keep her in the lifestyle she had always hankered after. It was not many months before Poppy received a letter saying she had married a Texan called Brad. He was quite a lot older than her, but mega-rich, of course. Now she was in the USA, living the American dream.

The subject was changed and Josh talked of people they'd known at school and what they were doing now. Then tales of who he'd bumped into at the rugby match in Launceston on Saturday. Bits of juicy local gossip from his gran were thrown in for good measure, even though Poppy hadn't a clue who most of the people were. Poppy listened as she cut off more chunks of cheese and ate, enjoying the warmth and ease she always felt in Josh's presence. But after he left, driving off down the uneven track, she felt unsettled and could not wait to get out of the silent cottage. She wanted to throw off that clinging, shuttered feeling. Quickly feeding Winston, she pulled on her walking boots and a coat, locked the door and tucked the key into her jeans' pocket. Poppy breathed in deeply, filling her lungs with sharp clear air. At that moment she almost felt alive again. She started to trudge down the lane which led on to the open moor.

'It was disgraceful of you. And on the Sabbath too,' came a man's pained voice.

A tantalising laugh was the reply. Poppy turned to see that she was not alone. A young woman with a beautiful face, of about twenty years at most, wearing an old-fashioned gown and a red cloth shawl, was picking her way gracefully through the mud, holding up her skirts. An unusual silk bonnet, with its ribbons flying free, framed her lovely face and she was laughing. Again, that tantalising laughter…

Poppy stood and stared, but they (for the woman had a male companion) came towards her down the lane and would soon be within touching distance. The woman's companion was just a few years older and his expression was clearly an unhappy one. His curly brown hair flopped over a pock-marked countenance and his mouth, in contrast, was turned down at the corners in sheer misery. His clothes, like the woman's, were old-fashioned. Yet the black frock-coat, breeches, white shirt and cravat tucked neatly into a rather fancy waistcoat gave the impression of a man who was wearing his best, doing his best even, to impress. However, he lurched as he walked, one leg seemingly shorter than the other. Nature had cursed him with a lame leg.

Poppy pressed herself back against the hedge. As they passed her she could even smell the mustiness of their clothes. The woman had looked straight at Poppy, smiling, yet it was obvious that she had not seen her. The couple made their way up the lane towards Higher Down Gate which led on to the moor. The man's voice was still plaintive, but Poppy could no longer hear his words. The response was further peals of girlish laughter. She started to follow this strange twosome up the lane, but suddenly realised they were no longer there. The muddied lane was deserted. The only sound was that of a buzzard high above screeching to its mate. Poppy turned and started to walk back towards the cottage. She felt as if her legs were about to give out. She had lost all sense of time. Where had she been? Who were the mismatched couple in their old-fashioned clothes?

Inside the cottage she poured herself a drink. Everything seemed normal enough. She looked out of the window at the sun sinking fast over the tors. Somewhere, out there on the vast moorland, a man and a woman were walking in their own time.

FOUR

WINSTON sat on the bed, rhythmically kneading the covers with his black paws, purring loudly. The radio alarm came on automatically and the strains of a romantic ballad filled the room.

Have I told you lately that I love you?

Van Morrison's distinctive gravelly tones. It was Sunday morning. Or was it? For out on the moor life seemed timeless.

'Yes, it's Sunday Love Songs,' thought Poppy. Memories of past Sunday mornings played on her mind. Sunday.

'It was disgraceful of you. And on the Sabbath too.'

The words spoken by the unhappy-looking man in the lane rang through her head. Who was he? And who was that enigmatic woman, with the tantalising laugh? Why had Poppy felt so disturbed to see them that her legs had almost given way beneath her? She fingered the silver cross nestling in the warm hollow of her neck. Matt's crucifix... taken from his body when he was found.

'Matt is dead. He killed himself.'

Those words knifed through her. That last winter they had rented a farmhouse at Morwenstow. While the gales rattled in from the Atlantic, Poppy had painted prolifically. There was an urgency to her work. She would wake early, in the darkness. The wind and rain would be smashing violently against the windows. The whole house would be shaking under the force of the storm. Winston would be curled up cosily on a mat in front of the Rayburn, indifferent to the storm outside. Poppy would drink cup after cup of black coffee. Then, still fatigued, in the watery morning light she would put luxuriant coloured paint on canvas with her palette knife. Some mornings it was as if she wanted to slap it on wildly, in empathy with the battle of the elements without the farmhouse walls. It became something of a compulsion then, despite having eyestrain in the poor light.

Matt, out of work, would stay in bed, sleep the mornings away. Then, bored, restless, he would walk the high, sheer cliffs in the wild grey afternoons of spray and thundering seas. Morwenstow cliffs were the scene of many shipwrecks. He would look down on the menacing rocks below and dwell on all those who had died there. In time Matt found a focus for his hours of emptiness. He became obsessed with finding out more about Parson Hawker, the legendary Vicar of Morwenstow who had lived in the vicarage in Victorian times. Hawker was generally thought to be an eccentric, striding the cliffs in his knitted fisherman's jersey, cassock and sea boots, looking for the bodies of drowned seamen. Then he would give them a proper Christian burial in the churchyard.

'Proper gruesome they say it were,' said Sam, an old local, nodding to Matt over a pint in The Bush Inn. 'Sometimes 'twas just limbs found between the rocks, arms and legs... then there were the corpses with no heads, because they'd been cut off by the jagged rocks! Gobbets of flesh too, lumps of it, all washed up by the sea.'

It was the stuff of nightmares.

'Have 'e seen the white monument in the churchyard, boy? Left of the path on your way down. Go and have a look for yourself. 'Tis the figurehead of a ship, the Caledonian. All died but one, and them're all buried here.'

Some locals were convinced that Hawker still haunted the churchyard, church and the cliffs.

'Oh yes. We see him now and again, walking up the churchyard path near the graves of all the sailors he rescued from the wrecks,' said Molly, one of the churchwardens, quite matter-of-factly.

'My dog won't go down that path if the old Parson be about,' nodded Sam over another free pint. 'Yet they do say 'e loved all animals. 'Twas Hawker who started off Harvest Festivals and he let folks bring their animals to the church with 'em.'

Matt took it all in and brooded on it in solitude. Some days he would just sit for hours on end in Hawker's Hut high on the cliffs. Originally built from driftwood dragged up from the beach below, this was Hawker's retreat from the world. It became Matt's retreat from reality too. Yet here in this simple shelter Hawker had been inspired to write poems and songs, scribble sermons, while smoking his pipes of opium. If opium was good enough for Parson Hawker, then a daily intake of cannabis might inspire him, Matt had thought. But there was no inspiration to follow. And then depression set in. Poppy rarely went out to the hut with Matt. She could not bear the dizzying height of the cliffs. In any case, she was too busy with her work. She had two commissions from a gallery-owner to finish and the deadlines were tight.

Matt felt lost and alone, angry about her absorption with painting. He felt resentful. Jealous, even, of her work. He knew it was crazy... and then he withdrew more and more into himself.

Looking back on it, Poppy realised just how much she had neglected Matt when he needed her most. But they had still loved one another, hadn't they? So why had he left her on her own? He would never hold her tightly in his arms again… and it was her fault. Waves of guilt washed over her as she pictured his broken body, as it had looked when he was found at the bottom of the cliffs below Hawker's Hut. Gulls wheeled and screamed above the foaming grey waters.

Once again Poppy told herself to stop thinking of his death. But she did not want to leave Matt behind. Little bits of him were already disappearing. She must learn to take one day at a time. Build some sort of life again.

For now it was a Sunday morning in April. Winston was settled and asleep on a pile of her clean clothes on the chair. And she was living on Bodmin Moor far away from Morwenstow on the north coast. Far away from the sea and the treacherous cliffs. Whatever happened, she must not give in to the nightmare of the past.

FIVE

IT was now mid-April and the moor was opening out to
the spring. The eternal wind blew across from the tors.
Their granite peaks were hidden in low cloud. She was
walking down the lane, the same lane as before, in its
comparative shelter. Just a few twisted trees on stony
hedges and a sea of mud. She came to the end of the lane
with no strange sightings as on the other occasion. Now
it was all open moorland, as far as Poppy could see.
There was not a human being in sight on the lonely
landscape, just white dots of sheep and lambs punctuated
the distance, grazing on the tough grass. Circling high
above, a pair of buzzards this time, screeching with their
distinctive call in the solitude.

Poppy made her way down a slope with only the
sound of a tumbling stream for company. She tramped
through broken stems of dead bracken and grass,
following the stream down, towards the ford at the foot
of Roughtor. Here the ground became softer, marshy.
Poppy's boots squelched and sucked through the boggy
ground. Somewhere in the distance a curlew's plaintive
cry echoed across the marshes. Shivering suddenly, she
turned up the collar of her old waxed jacket, looking up
towards the summits of Roughtor and Brown Willy,
which would be looming above her. The mist had
descended out of nowhere, shrouding the tors. Poppy
turned her head and saw that she was no longer alone in
the wilderness.

In front of her was the couple she'd seen in the lane
a few days ago. They were making their way along the

narrow track, which dipped towards the ford. They walked in single file and their progress was slow as the terrain was difficult and very wet in places. The man was stumbling in the wake of the pretty young woman, who was holding her skirts even higher above the boggy patches of moorland. Now and again her petticoats dipped in the water, for the going was difficult. Her bonnet was slightly askew now. Tendrils of shiny black hair framed her face, which kept turning towards the man struggling along behind her on his lame leg. She was smiling to herself. Or was she smiling back at Poppy? No, it was obvious that she had not seen her. A coldness crept over Poppy. The enveloping mist seemed to grow much colder.

The man with the strange gait and the somewhat hang-dog expression stopped to catch his breath. He seemed to be fixated on the woman ahead of him, watching her progress across the boggy ground with its mounds and tufts of grass. She turned back to him again and smiled. That enigmatic smile. Or was she laughing at his difficulty in walking?

'Matthew, I don't think you should come any further with me. 'Tis a bit misty as 'tis…and you'm so slow.'

Her tone of voice changed.

'And I have to meet up with Tommy Prout later at the Chapel.'

The man, Matthew, was clearly traumatised at her harsh words.

'But you promised to walk out with me today,' he said.

The woman stood impatiently on a grassy mound.

'I'm sorry Matthew… I don't want you. Go home.'

Then picking up her trailing skirts, she turned and dissolved into the mist. The woman had gone. And so had he.

An eerie silence settled on Roughtor marsh, broken only by the trickle of running water somewhere in the shivering reeds. Poppy felt freezing cold, her scalp icy. She croaked: 'Hello? Are you still there somewhere?'

The wind moaned a reply. Again the curlew cry haunted her. A fine drizzle started to roll down from the higher ground. She made an effort to pull herself together as she remembered how suddenly the Cornish weather could change. It was time to make her way back to the safety of her cottage. She turned to retrace her steps on to higher ground. The mist was closing in now, her wet hair jewelled with tiny droplets of water.

It was then she saw the woman once more. Walking as if out of the marshes. Alone now, shading her eyes as if looking for someone. Silently she passed by, neither turning her head nor acknowledging Poppy's presence. Again she shaded her eyes, for the dazzling sun was piercing the mist, searching that lonely landscape for someone or something. A bank of fog rolled across the sun and when it cleared Poppy saw that she was alone once again.

'Pull yourself together,' Poppy told herself, now trembling uncontrollably. 'Start walking, girl.'

She clambered hurriedly up the slope, slipping and sliding in the mud and wet grass. Gasping for breath (damn that bloody asthma), the muscles in her legs aching, her walking soon became laboured. She had been a fool to come so far from her cottage. But after what seemed an age, its familiar squat form with its tortured, twisted trees emerged from the mist. Poppy unlocked the door and slammed it heavily behind her. She thrust the heavy bolts across and leaned back against the worn oak. It felt solid. Friendly, behind her tense back.

Winston appeared, slinking down the stairs in the growing shadows of late afternoon. He rubbed against her legs. Sniffed her walking boots with their intriguing smell of marsh and bog-water. A deep purring rumbled from his throat. He was glad to see her. Poppy stooped to stroke him. Enjoyed the feeling of softness and warmth of the cat against her cold fingers. She bent down to take off her soaking boots. She pulled them off, feeling exhausted and dizzy. Her legs felt as if they would not hold her up. She leaned back against the white-washed wall. Her mind was reeling with snap-shot images... a woman in old-fashioned clothes walking through the mist... a petticoat dipping in muddy water... a beautiful face... tendrils of hair moving as if in a breeze. A woman turning her head, laughing...

What the hell was happening to her? She could not wait any longer. She needed a drink. With trembling hands she sloshed brandy into a glass, swirled it around the sides of the glass and drank.

SIX

THE fire had gone out in the hearth. The cottage felt cold and her bones ached. Poppy scrunched up an old newspaper and added dry sticks from a wicker basket. With trembling fingers she lit a match. It flared briefly in the afternoon gloom. Soon orange and red flames were flickering and twigs were crackling. She held her hands out to the warmth. If only Matt was here to hold her close. To feel his body heat. Listen to his heart beating.

But Matt was not here. He was dead. And now he was dust.

Ashes to ashes.

Dust to dust.

The flames leaped higher. Shadows flickered on the rough walls. She pulled off her damp jacket with its distinctive waxy smell and wriggled her aching shoulders. She lit the brass oil lamp that they had bought together at a junk shop on the Barbican at Plymouth. Its mellow light brought colour and cheer to the living-room.

Winston padded noiselessly towards the fire and sat on the bright woollen rug. Poppy watched as he washed himself. He settled, made himself comfortable and closed his eyes. She envied him his equanimity. She peered out of the window, leaning on her elbows as she craned her neck. The intense hyacinth perfume made her head spin. Outside, the drizzling rain had ceased but the wind was getting up. It was moving the branches of the trees, silver-grey in the light of late afternoon. Poppy still felt uneasy as if she was being watched. The gate in the lichened stone wall had been pushed open and now it was swinging violently. She pulled the heavy curtains to shut out the onset of a dreary evening. The room was much warmer and soon soporific music flooded the room. Poppy made a cup of tea and sipped it pensively. She could hear the wind beginning its melancholy moan outside and now and again a gust came down the chimney. She felt she ought to eat something as she could feel the effects of the brandy. She forced herself to eat some hot buttered toast and put more wood on the fire. She picked up her worn copy of *Wuthering Heights* and curled up in the comfy armchair. She smiled to think of Josh's comment about Heathcliff that he'd made on their first viewing of the cottage. More relaxed now, she began to read. But the walk across the moor had taken its toll. She felt exhausted. Soon her head started to loll drowsily against the cushions in the warmth. Her eyes gradually closed…

'… still heard the gusty wind and the tapping on the window of a branch. A melancholy voice sobbed, 'Let me in. I've lost my way on the moor…' A face was looking through the window…'

Poppy woke in a frenzy of panic, screaming aloud. The room was too hot now. Much too hot. Sweat drenched her armpits and beaded her forehead. The tranquil music had finished. Her book had slipped on to the rug by the fireside and its pages were dog-eared. A log shifted and fell with a shower of tiny sparks. She had been dreaming, surely? She sat up stiffly, the drops of sweat rapidly cooling on her skin. Outside the wind was howling around the walls of the cottage. Twigs were scratching, tapping at the window.

'Get a grip, girl.'

She must force herself to look out of the window.

Poppy yanked back the curtains. They screeched on their brass rings. Night, like an intruder, entered the cottage and with it, terror. The white face of a woman, the woman she had seen down by the marshes that afternoon, was looking through the window. The twisted branches of a tree rattled against the glass panes.

'I became lost on the moors... tell Matthew that I have gone to Blisland.'

Her words were ripped away by the wind's blast... 'Tell him not to come after me again.'

Then she turned away from the window and disappeared into the darkness. Poppy was transfixed, staring into the night, trembling with the terror of it all. Her hands were ice-cold. She reached to drag the curtains across once more, to shut out the darkness and whatever it held. She fumbled for her mobile phone and scrolled through the names with shaking hands. Josh. Josh would come. She knew that she could rely on him to come, whatever he was doing. The signal was poor, but he sensed the panic in her voice. What a gibbering wreck she must sound.

'I'm on my way Poppy. Stay inside 'til I get to you.'

Josh drove his old jeep like a maniac down the narrow, winding lanes. He had been born locally and knew every bend and dip along the way. At last he saw the yellow square of light belonging to Penhale Cottage. Trees were silhouetted against the tiny window, their branches thrashing in torment. Poppy was crouching by the fire on the rug, hugging her knees and nursing a huge brandy, when she heard Josh grating his gears outside. She ran to unlock the door and flung herself into his solid, comforting hug. He drew her back into the warmth of the cottage and shut the door on the storm. Josh was shocked when he saw her anguished and tearful face.

'Ssh... it's all right, Poppy. I'm here now, you're

safe,' he said, stroking her hair like one might do to a child. He rocked her in his muscular arms and she breathed in his familiar smell, a mixture of hay and male muskiness. His sheer size and strength comforted her, calmed her. Sobbing, barely coherent, she blurted out an account of her experience of seeing a strange couple out on the moor, and later at her window the same woman's face, ghostly-pale. It all seemed a childish tale now that Josh was actually here with her and she broke away from him. He must think her hysterical and silly. She blew her nose noisily and knelt by the fire. Winston had vacated his place on the mat when the door had opened and he'd heard a deep voice. Now he watched the happenings from the safety of the stairs.

'You probably think I'm going crazy,' said Poppy quietly.

SEVEN

JOSH moved towards her in the flickering firelight. He couldn't help loving her. She looked so vulnerable, her white hand shaking as she drained her brandy glass. He wanted to hold her again, he felt *he* was going out of his mind, not Poppy. Seeing her like this made him feel so miserable and despairing. She spoke again, looking up at him.

'I'm not going crazy Josh. It really happened. You must believe me!'

'Of course you're not going crazy. But for all that it's not doing you much good being out here on your own like this.'

He bent to pick up the discarded book from the rug. Its pages were crumpled and creased. He held it out towards her.

'Jesus, Poppy! Reading *Wuthering Heights* yet again won't bloody help!'

He flicked the worn pages.

'Think about it Poppy... it's about a young woman who returns to haunt her obsessive lover in an isolated farmhouse on the moor. It's got into your head, that's all. You must have dozed off and had a nightmare. It's as simple as that.'

She shook her head vehemently and faced him.

'No, Josh. This was no Cathy Linton in a work of fiction. It happened just as I said. All of it. From the encounter down near Roughtor ford, to the tapping at the window and then her face tonight. You must believe me. It's all true, I swear.'

She bent over and jabbed viciously at the burning logs with a poker. Josh rolled a cigarette expertly and offered it to Poppy. She shook her head again.

'No thanks.'

He lit the cigarette himself and it glowed red as he drew on it.

'But another brandy would be nice.'

Her voice was almost back to normal now. He poured the brandy for her, noting that the bottle was only about a third full. Another brandy bottle, already empty, stood by the stone sink.

'Here.'

He handed Poppy the brandy goblet and she cupped it in her hands.

'You're drinking rather a lot of the hard stuff.'

Josh squatted on his haunches next to her on the hearth.

'Getting totally pissed won't help.'

She turned her gaze from the fire to Josh. Her green eyes glittered dangerously.

'I'm not drunk, if that's what you think. And it's not my imagination. I'm not seeing things.'

She looked at the flames.

'There *is* a woman somewhere out there, walking on the moors.'

Her voice was emphatic. Josh stood up and pulled aside the curtain. He stared out at the thrashing branches and the gate, still swinging on its hinges. The wind moaned around the walls of granite, like a soul in torment. He wrenched the curtain close to obliterate the darkness out there and faced her.

'Look, I'm staying the night here with you.'

She opened her mouth to protest.

'It's no good bloody arguing Poppy! I'm not leaving you here alone tonight. I'll sleep down here by the fire.'

There was no further argument. The brandy was dulling her fears, warming her, making her relax. They gathered cushions and a sleeping bag and made a nest. Winston crept down the stairs out of the shadows and watched them balefully. They sat by the fire together and talked. Josh drank a couple of beers. His generous, weathered face showed his concern for her. There was a solidity about Josh that was reassuring, not just his rugby-player's shoulders and muscular physique. She felt a sense of peace with him there at her side. The woman on the marshes dissolved from Poppy's mind, just as she had dissolved into the mist. The fire was dying down and only a reddish glow remained. Her eyelids felt heavy.

Exhausted, she leaned back against his arm. Josh looked down at her sleeping face. He was happy just to look at her. Her skin clear and white, her closed eyelids hiding her eyes like green glass flecked with hazel lights. Her red hair a tangled bird's nest. To him she was extraordinarily beautiful, although she would say, as she often had done before, she hated her large mouth. Ugly, is how she always described it. He stared meditatively at the glowing embers of the fire. His arm had the beginnings of cramp. He was uncomfortable, but he would not move for fear of disturbing Poppy. He was aching to kiss her. He closed his eyes. He remembered how jealous he had felt when Poppy had fallen for Matt. He was ashamed of it now. For Matt was dead... and here he was, very much alive, with the girl he loved asleep in his arms.

Josh must have dozed for a while. When he opened his eyes again and looked at her, he was only aware that his normal coolness and self-control had evaporated. Decisively he pulled Poppy towards him and kissed her. Just for a short while her instincts took over. She arched her body up against him and kissed him back. She shivered as her body responded to Josh. Sexual feelings of desire were briefly set in motion. But then memory kicked in. Memories of Matt and her absolute grief for his loss hit her. Shocked, she pulled back from Josh's kiss. She scrambled to her feet. Eyes glittering, her face was pale as death. Josh was distraught. He too struggled to his feet, rubbing his cramped arm.

'I'm sorry. I just can't pretend any longer to be just mates, Poppy! You know how I feel about you. I just want to be there for you. To look after you.'

His familiar face looked haunted, his dark blue eyes staring at her.

'I'm really sorry... I've spoilt it all.'

Poppy could feel the chill penetrating her body. She could not look at him. There was a moment when everything stopped. She felt she could not even breathe. Josh stood like a statue of stone. She threw some dry twigs on to the embers and watched them catch alight, spitting and crackling. She knew how much Josh had suffered because of her over the years. She knew only too well how he had always been there, even at school, to listen to her problems. It had been Josh who had dropped everything and rushed to Morwenstow in those terrible days after losing Matt. And now in a moment everything had changed between them. She turned to him, slowly.

'It's not your fault Josh,' she said in a low voice. 'I've been so selfish. It's not your fault that I can't leave Matt behind.'

She hesitated, her voice barely audible.

'And I don't deserve someone like you to love me. I just keep on giving you a hard time and making you unhappy.'

'I can cope,' Josh's voice managed a croak. He

gazed at her exhausted white face. 'Look, it's late. You ought to get some sleep. It's been a tough day.'

She climbed the stairs slowly and with a heavy heart. Up to her lonely bedroom and empty bed. Josh sat by the remains of the fire, staring at its glowing embers, chain-smoking with trembling hands. He knew that he loved Poppy dearer than life. But their kiss had been snuffed out, like a candle, all too quickly.

'How the hell can I make her love me, when she's in love with Matt's ghost?'

It was many hours before sleep came to him.

EIGHT

THE morning light began to creep into the cottage. Josh stirred and opened his eyes. The hearth was grey with ashes. He was lying on the rug in a sleeping-bag. He stared up at the old beams above him and thought of the people who had once lived there. Tough, moorland folk. Wild and earthy. The personification of the moor itself, they would have lived in tune with the seasons and fought to survive. He thought of all the babies born under that very roof, and of those who had died there. His thoughts turned to the night before and trawled through the sequence of events. Poppy had panicked earlier that evening, but what had really caused it? Her voice had triggered something in him, making him drive like some kind of lunatic to her side even more quickly than usual. Then at her most vulnerable there had been his fumbled kiss... what a mess he'd made of it all.

Quietly, but very stiffly, he got up and stretched his arms. He pulled aside the curtain. Outside it was a lovely spring morning, the wind had dropped overnight and the sun's slanting rays bathed the open moorland in mellow light. It was a scene of tranquillity. Josh filled the kettle and the drumming sound made Poppy stir upstairs. She opened her eyes and felt how good it was to hear the movements of another human being. Then, as always, her heart ached for Matt. His portrait was looking at her from the foot of the bed, his eyes sad and lost. What would he say to her if he were here now? But he was not here. She suddenly thought of his ashes, still at the undertaker's waiting for her to pick them up. She lay back against the pillows and closed her eyes again. In her mind she too went over the happenings of the evening before. What must Josh think of her? He had dropped everything at a moment's notice and rushed to her rescue, probably causing problems at their farm. God knows what his parents must think of her. Then, later, she had hissed at him like some kind of Harpy when he clumsily tried to kiss her by the fire. Poor Josh... it was true, she did not deserve him.

'Here you are, a strong cup of tea.'

Josh put it on her bedside table.

'And now I'm going to make you a bacon sandwich.'

Before Poppy could even open her mouth to reply, he'd started back down the stairs. The smell of bacon frying soon wafted up from below. Poppy luxuriated, guiltily, in the feeling of being pampered as she sipped her tea. She got out of her bed (it was Matt's bed too but she must not think of that) and looked out of the tiny casement window. Sunlight was streaming through the panes. The terrors of the night had been brushed away and the landscape was breathtakingly beautiful. Poppy took off the crumpled clothes she'd slept in and grabbed some clean ones. Her head ached (that was the brandy) and she probably looked like Sal Hatch, whoever she was.

She smiled at the Cornish expression as she dragged a brush through her tangled hair. She was desperate to wash and brush her teeth. Her tongue felt furry. Trying not to trip over Winston, who was watching the bacon-frying with his usual look of disdain, she went down the stairs. No mention was made of the night before.

'Today we're going out somewhere.'

Josh gave her no choice.

'So, eat your breakfast up. It'll do you good.'

He could not help noticing her prominent collar-bones.

'You still look far too bloody thin, like David Beckham's missus on a bad day!'

Poppy knew he was right. It had been months since she had eaten properly. Her face was gaunt and her jeans were hanging off her. Half an hour later they climbed into Josh's muddy jeep and turned their backs on the moors.

'Where are we going?' Poppy asked as they drove past Davidstow church.

'Just look at the signposts and you'll see,' Josh grinned.

It was not long before the blue sea appeared, its white horses stampeding on to slate-black cliffs. Poppy's spirits lifted. The jeep started its descent towards Boscastle.

'I haven't been here since the terrible floods,' said Poppy, peering out of the jeep's dirt-spattered window as Josh navigated the infamous hair-pin bend. Below them was the harbour, but the picture was much changed. Gone was the quaint Harbour Light building with its sloping roof and arched windows. It was here that Poppy had been entranced by all the pixies as a child. She felt that another little piece of her childhood had been taken away. She could see her mother now, sitting across the river on the other bank looking bored. Then she pictured her harassed father as he queued for ice-creams, promising to look at the pixies yet again with a persistent Poppy. Her darling father. And now he was gone. Had she really known how difficult things had been for him? Her mother had never been satisfied. There was never enough money. Was she ever happy? Her father had gone into a decline after Poppy's mother divorced him. And then he'd become ill. And that was it. He'd just given up.

'Poppy! Did you hear a word I was saying?'

Josh's voice crashed in on her thoughts.

'Sorry. I was miles away.'

'I said, what about going for a pint and a pasty at the Cobweb Inn?'

Josh was pulling into the car park as he spoke. He wrenched up the hand brake.

'Fine,' she nodded.

How on earth she could manage to eat a pasty after bacon sandwiches for breakfast she could not imagine.

'Can we walk down to the harbour first?'

They meandered like a couple of tourists by the stream, now sparkling in the sunshine.

'It's hard to imagine the raging torrent isn't it?'

The Museum of Witchcraft had been freshly painted, ready for the Easter influx of holiday-makers. Boscastle was showing signs of life once more. They crossed the bridge under which cars had become wedged in the roaring black floodwaters. Then sauntered down towards the ancient harbour. They climbed the cliffs and looked down at the water below them. They paused to listen to the booming of the blow-hole. Poppy had spots of colour in her cheeks for the first time in weeks, Josh noticed.

'About last night,' said Poppy, her voice quiet.

'You don't have to talk about it if you don't want to,' Josh replied.

'Ah but I do want to talk about it, Josh. You were brilliant coming out to my rescue like that, but it hasn't gone away. I can still see that woman's face at the window.'

Poppy looked out to sea.

'She was very beautiful, very pale. She looked so... so incredibly sad.'

'I know someone who looks like that,' Josh interrupted, squeezing her arm.

'I'm being serious. Who can she be?'

She turned to face him.

'Well it's not Catherine Earnshaw, that's for sure!'

Josh pulled her coat.

'Come on. Let's walk back to the pub. We could call in on my gran later, seeing we're in Boscastle. Could you bear that?'

'Of course I could bear it. I love your gran. She's a real character,' said Poppy, smiling.

'Actually I reckon she's one of the original Boscastle witches.'

Josh pointed to the Museum of Witchcraft across the stream. Poppy remembered, vaguely, a photo being taken of her in front of its fascinating exterior by her father. Where was that photo now, she wondered. Possibly in the box with faded postcards and letters she'd rescued from his bedroom in a nostalgic moment.

'Come on then,' Josh urged. She let herself be ushered into the dark interior of the Cobweb Inn.

NINE

AFTER the bright spring sunshine Poppy's eyes took a few minutes to become accustomed to the gloom. Old wooden settles on huge slate slabs, dusty bottles and jars hanging from ancient beams, yellowing photos of local people and places, the Cobweb was a traditional Cornish pub. Josh was greeted with immediate warmth by a couple of old locals leaning on the bar.

'Right boy? 'ow be 'e?'

Josh's hand was shaken strongly by gnarled, brown hands. He stood and chatted animatedly (probably about tractors and livestock, thought Poppy) whilst she slid into the seat of a tall settle. She could look around, unnoticed, from her dark corner. The pints were bought and pasties ordered. Josh brought her drink over and retreated to the male domain of the bar once more to finish his conversation. She sipped her beer and her eyes travelled around the room. The flashing lights of a fruit machine seemed incongruous here. The outside door opened and two girls came in, laughing. They brought light and life with them. One was dressed in bright, vivid colours with lots of jangling jewellery and with spiky hair, but she was eclipsed by the tall girl at her side who was simply stunning. They clattered to the bar on noisy high-heeled boots.

'Josh Clemo. I can't believe it!' shrieked the dumpier of the two.

'Josh. Where have you been for so long?'

The other one's voice was lower, smooth as velvet.

From her nook Poppy could see Josh being

smothered with hugs and kisses. Who was that lovely girl? And why, asked Poppy, did she feel so annoyed by her Josh's friendliness with her? She shrank back into her dark corner and drank from the pint of beer, wishing it were a glass of wine. Josh and the girls were laughing and chatting by the bar, seemingly oblivious to her presence. A sheep-dog came in from the other bar; it wagged its tail at Poppy and then settled at her feet, its head between its paws. Hot pasties duly arrived. Josh abandoned the bar and went over to Poppy. He seemed very pleased with himself, she thought. His freckled face was positively glowing as he picked up his pasty and took great bites from it. Poppy toyed with her food. She was not hungry. She pushed crumbs of pastry around her plate. Josh motioned to her to eat, but she could not face it.

'She's very pretty,' she said, sipping her beer.

Josh seemed not to hear this and swigged heavily from his glass.

'I said, she's very pretty,' Poppy persisted, hating herself.

'Who? Oh, you mean Lowenna.' Josh wiped his wet mouth. 'I suppose she is. Never really thought about it,' he shrugged.

Shrieks of laughter came from the bar. Poppy looked down at her plate.

'You obviously don't fancy that, so let's go,' said Josh, grimacing at the mangled pasty in front of Poppy.

As she squeezed out of her tight spot in the corner, she was aware of a hostile glance from the lovely Lowenna.

'Bye Josh. See you soon,' came honeyed tones.

Outside the pub the sunlight was blinding. Josh steered her across the road to his jeep. They drove up the hill from the harbour to the top of Boscastle village, well away from the river. Talk was difficult, there was an atmosphere between them that needed dispelling. Josh's gran, Gweniver, lived in a quaint white cottage with Gothic windows. She had been a widow for donkeys years. In fact Josh could not really remember his grandfather, just a vague recollection of the smell of a pipe and seaman's boots.

'Well I'm darned. You've actually brought Poppy to see me!'

A bent-backed tiny Cornishwoman, Gweniver was still very much full of life.

'Well don't just stand there, come on in you two. I'll put the kettle on.'

A wonderful smell of saffron permeated the room. They sipped strong tea and Josh ate saffron buns obligingly. When Poppy could not be tempted, Josh's gran told her: 'You need feeding up, maid. You'm just skin and bone!'

Poppy's wan smile in response provoked further comment.

'And you'm as pale as a white-washed wall. You look like you've seen a ghost.'

Josh coughed in an embarrassed manner and looked out of the window.

'I think I may have,' said Poppy, barely audible.

In no time at all Gweniver had ferreted out the tale of Poppy's strange sightings on the moor and, later, at her window in the darkness the day before. Her gimlet eyes gleamed knowingly at the mention of Roughtor ford.

'Charlotte Dymond herself... that's who you saw.'

Gweniver nodded her silver head. Josh snorted in derision.

'Charlotte Dymond? What, you mean the girl who was murdered on the moors all those years ago?'

Poppy's eyes widened.

'I remember reading the ballad at school. Charles Causley wrote it. She was killed by her lover, wasn't she?'

'That's right,' Gweniver nodded again. 'Matthew Weeks. He were hanged at Bodmin a few months after, poor boy. He weren't very bright they say. Couldn't read nor write a word. Folk on the moor used to say he were too easily led off to the gallows.'

Gweniver drained her tea-cup.

'Charlotte's mother were a Boscastle maid herself, a school teacher. Brought shame and disgrace on 'er family when 'er gave birth to Charlotte. Illegitimate child. Different in them days. As soon as 'twas humanly possible, Charlotte was put in service on a farm over to Davidstow parish.'

Poppy, on the edge of her seat, looked across at Josh, who was trying to stop his gran, now in full flow.

'Your gran's making a lot of sense, Josh. The woman at the window mentioned the name Matthew... she said to tell him not to keep on following her.'

Poppy reflected.

'Then she said something about going to Blisland.'

'So 'er was... but 'er never got there. Charlotte's body were found down in the marsh, days after 'er went missing, 'er throat 'ad been cut.'

Gweniver paused.

'Before long, Matthew were arrested at Plymouth and brought back to Bodmin Gaol. Local farmers 'ad seen Matthew on the moor with Charlotte near Roughtor. So they said. But 'tis many years ago.'

There was a moment's silence, all of them absorbed in the echoes of the tragic past. Josh looked at his watch and stood up suddenly. His chair scraped on the floor.

'Thanks for the tea Gran, but we must be off now.

Things to do at Poppy's cottage.'

Gweniver looked at her grandson shrewdly.

'Well don't do anything daft, Joshua.'

Then to an ashen-faced Poppy: 'Drop in any time dear, I'm always glad of the company.'

Josh's jeep bumped its way along the lane leading to Penhale. There was an angry frown in place of his usual smile.

'My gran's a silly old woman, telling you all that morbid stuff in your frame of mind. P'raps we should have gone to Padstow instead and had fish and chips.'

Poppy's cottage was around the next bend. It didn't look at all grim in the sunshine. She was almost glad to be back. The jeep bumped up on to the grass verge.

'I must get back to the farm and put in a few hours work, at least.'

Josh rolled a cigarette slowly. He did not want to leave her.

'I'll be back later on.'

He paused.

'You will be OK, won't you?'

Poppy smiled. She felt stronger again.

'Of course I will. Thanks Josh.'

She gave him a hug and climbed out of the jeep. She turned her back on him and put a key in the lock. Yes, she felt stronger. She looked back at the open moorland surrounding her cottage and mused on Gweniver's words. Poppy resolved to visit Bodmin, with its notorious old gaol, the very next day.

TEN

IT was drizzling as Poppy's car descended the old coach road into a grey, wet Bodmin. Had she but known it, this was the very route that the Assize Judge would have travelled back in 1844 on his arduous journey from Exeter to Bodmin, to try the case of Matthew Weeks for murder.

Poppy drove down Castle Hill, negotiating the bend before the beautiful old church. She remembered her father telling her St Petroc's Church was the largest parish church in Cornwall on one of their visits to an aunt who lived in the former county town. She parked her car near Priory Park pond, where the ducks were enjoying the wet weather, quacking loudly as they fought for sodden bits of bread thrown from an elderly lady in a glistening mac. Rain pattered more heavily on the rhododendron leaves which grew in profusion around the pond, shutting it in from the world of cars and the sound of traffic.

Wrestling with a broken umbrella, Poppy crossed the car park in the direction of the shops and cafes. A cup of strong black coffee suddenly seemed very appealing, and perhaps a hot sausage roll. Half an hour later, much replenished, Poppy retraced her steps. Rain splashed in the puddles and her head was bent under the umbrella. On her right now, up the steps, was the impressive Shire Hall, built of granite and previously Bodmin Assize Court. This then, was where Matthew Weeks had been tried for the murder of Charlotte Dymond.

As she climbed the steps and entered the foyer, her

stomach turned to water and her legs started to tremble. A woman with a mass of grey hair loosely piled on top of her head smiled at her encouragingly from behind a rack of guidebooks and tourist information leaflets.

'Hello. Can I help you?'

The woman smiled again. Poppy felt dizzy, nauseous. Bright lights flashed and the woman's lip-sticked mouth and teeth seemed suddenly huge. A hubbub of sound grew out of nowhere, growing louder and louder. It was hot, so incredibly hot that Poppy wrenched off her soaking wet coat. The twisted umbrella with its broken spokes fell to the floor...

A man's voice could be heard saying, 'It's terrible hot today,' as he rolled up his sleeves, 'but then 'tis August after all!' He mopped his brow.

'I wouldn't miss this for anything though,' came an older croaky voice.

Poppy stared as a noisy crowd jostled and fought through the open doorway. She had the impression of a mass of sweating, unwashed bodies cramming into the entrance vestibule. There was a sense of panic in their wild eyes. She could even feel their foul breath on her face as they pushed past her into the court-room. It was obvious they had not seen her.

'Out of my way! Get out of my way!' yelled a huge man wearing some kind of antiquated official uniform. He seemed to glare straight at Poppy as she pressed herself back against the stone wall. He shouldered his way through the crowd. A gaunt-faced man with a beard and wearing a gold chain looped on his black waistcoat followed in his wake, attempting to retain some sort of dignity in the chaos. He clasped a sheaf of papers closely to his chest, protecting them from the melee which surrounded him.

'That's that there solicitor from Lanson,' shouted the

man next to Poppy, still mopping his brow with a neckerchief. 'He's defending the murderer.'

The older man croaked, gleefully: 'He've got 'is work cut out for 'en then, we all do knaw Weeks is guilty!'

She listened as the mob crowded through the arched doorway of the granite-faced building. They had all come with one purpose, to watch a drama unfold within the Assize Hall. They were determined to force their way through into the packed Crown Court.

'I d'reckon there's as many folk in Bodmin today as four years ago, when them Lightfoot brothers were on trial,' shouted the brow-mopper, above the din.

'That were a good 'anging! Two brothers swinging on the rope at the same time,' said the older man, relishing the memory. The macabre comment and the stifling heat made Poppy's head spin. She felt hemmed in by the dizzying swirl of women in long summer dresses and shawls, confused by the leering faces of men with broken teeth in the mob. Bile rose from her stomach and she fought it down. The crowd surged past her, some openly fighting in their desperation to cram into the already-crowded room. An unkempt woman in a stained apron screamed and fell and only the police constables saved her from being trampled to death. The heat and crush of bodies was becoming unbearable.

Constables and court officials, dressed in black, cleared the entrance, restoring order for the procession of the barristers and the formidable-looking judge. He held a scented handkerchief to his nose, as he stood within touching distance of Poppy. She flinched as he turned his head in her direction and met the stare of his steely-grey eyes. She felt the coldness there... yet it was clear that he did not actually see her, flattened as she was against the stone wall.

An official bellowed: 'All stand for the case of Regina versus Weeks.'

The sombre procession filed into the courtroom. A screech of heavy metal bolts being drawn back echoed around the entrance hall. A door opened, revealing stone steps down to the holding cells from where a terrible stench wafted up. Poppy gagged. Once more she tasted vomit in her mouth. A sullen-looking man with curly brown hair was led up from the cells by two grim warders. The prisoner, dressed in a jacket of blue cloth and a fancy waistcoat limped towards the dock. The rows of glass buttons on his waistcoat glinted as they took on the light. He looked up from under his over-hanging brows and there was a faint suggestion of a lop-sided grimace on his face.

Poppy remembered that expression. The last time she had seen the prisoner, he had been walking down the lane from Penhale Farm with the tantalising young woman who had told him quite clearly: 'I'm sorry Matthew, I don't want you. Go home.'

She remembered the pain and suffering etched in his pock-marked face; then the intense heat, gathering black dots and specks of light overtook her and she slithered to the floor.

ELEVEN

WHEN Poppy opened her eyes she was sitting on the floor of the foyer, feeling a complete fool. The woman with the mass of tumbling grey hair was kneeling next to her, holding a glass to her mouth and attempting to get her to sip some water. Poppy leaned her head forward and reached for the glass. Her hand trembled and drops of water splashed on to the stone floor.

'Let me hold that before you drop it dear,' the woman smiled. 'Like a cup of tea instead?'

'No, no thanks. I'm fine now. I was just a bit faint.'

She scrambled clumsily to her feet.

'Need some air. Can't breathe. It's all these people, it's too bloody claustrophobic,' she said, making for the doorway of the Shire Hall.

'Which people, dear?'

Poppy could see the hordes of people were no longer with her. Except for a little old man in a wet raincoat looking at postcards on a rack, the hall was empty. She realised, too, that she had abandoned her own wet coat and broken umbrella and the rain was pouring down on the Folly outside. After the intense heat and crush inside the Assize Court she shivered with the cold as she stood on the granite steps. Her drenched clothes clung to her. Her hair stuck to her neck with moisture.

'Nipples like chapel hat-pegs!'

Poppy turned to see the old man in the raincoat leering at her before he hurried off across the Folly in the April rain.

'Pervert!' she yelled loudly and was ashamed to see

an elderly lady stop to stare at her from under her dripping brolly. Poppy stood there in the rain, not knowing where she was or in what time. A postman started to climb the Shire Hall steps carrying a large parcel. He stared at her. A look of recognition passed between them.

'Poppy Trewen? What the hell are you doing here in Bodmin? You're absolutely soaked.'

He grinned at her and ushered her out of the rain, under cover of the arched doorway.

'You don't remember me?'

She twisted in embarrassment and confusion.

'Yes... I mean I think so,' she replied.

'Wait here while I dump this parcel. I'm Steve, a mate of Josh. We met one Christmas in Lanson.'

Her mind whirling, Poppy thought back to a rather drunken Christmas Eve. The square at Launceston had been heaving with people, and the pubs too. She had been home from college and she had been with Josh and a crowd of friends. It had been in the days before she met Matt. She recalled the lounge bar being too hot. There was a sea of faces crowding together, most of them familiar. It was a happy, festive occasion. Loud laughter filled the room. Drinks were pouring down throats at a furious rate and the atmosphere was blue with smoke. Josh arrived late with two of his friends in tow. One was thin and weazly, a chain-smoker with a nervous twitch under one eye. The other was Steve. He looked different now, in his postman's uniform. Then, his hard muscles had been on display, even on a cold evening in December. She remembered more clearly how his roving, twinkling blue eyes had swept the room. She remembered too how she had indulged in a few silly kisses under the mistletoe with him, until he disappeared with a pretty blonde. Much later he'd reappeared looking extremely pleased with himself and received drunken ribbing from the crowd.

Now it was a miserable day in Bodmin, the rain was still pouring as Poppy waited, wet and shivering. Waiting for what, she asked herself. But she felt drained after her experience in the courtroom and she had no direction.

'Sorry about that,' said Steve. 'Let's go somewhere so you can dry off.'

She still felt confused and a bit wobbly. She was glad of a friendly face and someone to tell her what to do and where to go.

'Come back to my place,' Steve invited her with a dazzling smile that brought back memories of mistletoe and wine. Poppy nodded weakly and allowed him to take her through the April rain to his car. She got inside gratefully and slumped in the front seat.

'I'm renting a place at Hillside Park with some mates,' he grinned, 'but they're away in Ibiza looking for some early sun and some action.'

He started the engine and switched on the wipers. Sheets of water ran off the windscreen. A quick drive around the ring-road and the car turned down a precipitous hill and into a council estate. Houses like boxes were ranged on each side. Poppy thought of her granite cottage on the moor and yearned for it. Below Hillside in the valley stood Bodmin Gaol, dark and gloomy in the relentless rain. A mad dash into the house and Poppy found herself shivering in a small, untidy sitting-room. Steve put the kettle on and made coffee for them both while he chattered away, not seeming to notice the monosyllabic replies to his questions. He cleared away a pile of magazines and papers from a worn sofa.

'Sit down and make yourself at home, while I get this uniform off.'

He jogged upstairs, whistling to himself tunelessly.

Poppy cupped her coffee in both hands, wondering how on earth she had ended up in this place. Her head hurt and she was still wet and cold. She stood up and went over to the window. She drew aside the voile curtains. Raindrops trickled down the panes but she could see the gaol clearly with its rows of little dark windows dominated by its grim tower.

'That's better.'

Steve's voice made her jump. He had changed into a pair of faded black jeans and was pulling a sweatshirt over his muscles.

'Why don't you take that wet t-shirt off?' he smiled, blue eyes twinkling in a way she now remembered well, 'You can borrow one of mine.'

His hands were on her shoulders, travelling up her neck, stroking her wet hair and pale face. He bent his head and kissed her. She turned away from him.

'Please don't, Steve,' she murmured, struggling away rather feebly. 'I really don't feel well.'

'Come on Poppy, you know you want to really,' he smirked. He kissed her again, roughly this time so that she could not breathe. His arm-muscles tightened around her like a vice and he pushed her down on to the sofa. Disorientated, weakened, she could not fight him off physically. Even a knee in the groin would not stop him.

'Get off me!'

She had to think quickly.

'I've got bloody chlamydia!' she shrieked at him.

The vice-like grip loosened instantly. The heavy breathing in her ear ceased. She lay motionless. When she opened her eyes he was standing by the window with his back to her. She was lying awkwardly, half on the sofa, half on the floor. The window was a grey square of watery light. Raindrops trickled down it like tears.

TWELVE

LIKE an automaton she got up from the floor. 'I need the loo,' she heard her own voice say, as if it was underwater. 'It's upstairs on the right.' He did not meet her eyes. Poppy staggered up the stairs and into the bathroom. Moments later all the nausea welled up. She vomited noisily into the lavatory. She felt dirty, betrayed. She swilled her mouth out with water and looked at herself in the mirror with self-loathing. She made a decision there and then that no one must ever know what had nearly happened. Especially Josh. Half an hour later she was back in her own car at Priory Park. Steve had made a half-hearted attempt at an apology.

'But I honestly thought that was what you wanted,' his voice trailed off. He saw the contempt in her cold eyes of glittering, green glass. Then he'd driven off in a cloud of black exhaust fumes. She watched him go in her driving-mirror.

'Bastard!'

She slumped over the steering wheel, gripping it with both hands tightly. What an idiot she'd been, to trust someone like him. How naive, to believe he would help her in her confused state at the Shire Hall. He was a brute. By the time he'd he got back to his seedy house at Hillside he'd have forgotten all about her…

The rain had stopped now and a watery sun shone over the car park. Metallic gleams shone across the tarmac. She put the car window down and breathed in the freshness of rain on grass and vegetation. It made her feel a little better. She put the key in the ignition and started the engine. It was time to get home. She needed a shower and to put the whole bloody experience behind her. She drove across the open moor towards Blisland and St Breward with her car windows open, the wind blowing hard as she reached higher ground. Moorland horses and ponies cropped the grass on the verges of the narrowing track.

Ahead of her were the tors bathed in light. The only sounds were of the wind whistling across the rough pasture and the bleating of sheep and lambs. It was good to turn her back on so-called civilisation and feel she could breathe again.

Back at her cottage she was welcomed by Winston, rubbing against her legs and purring loudly. She opened a tin of cat food and set it down for him. Then she piled dry sticks into the hearth and lit a fire. She squatted by the hearth, stuffing bits of rolled-up newspaper into the leaping flames and added more twigs and a couple of bone-dry logs. She stood in the shower and let rivulets of water stream over her head and body, scrubbing herself with a rough loofah, desperate to feel clean again. Pure smells of lemon and orange blossom filled the air. Into her head came a voice.

'Put it out of mind, Poppy. You are stronger than this. It was not even sex, thank God. It was not important.'

She massaged shampoo into her hair.

'Think of the times as an art student when you woke up next to men you hardly knew, tousled heads on the pillow and a feeling of instant regret. Just put this down to experience, a bloody awful experience. Blank it out.'

But then from nowhere Matt's face appeared in her mind, shaking his head in disbelief, those remarkable eyes so sad as he gazed at her. Poppy was shivering now as she emerged from the shower. She bundled her hair up into a towel and rubbed herself dry, hating herself. She pulled on a comforting old chenille dressing-gown and made a hot drink. Sitting by the fire she stroked Winston's beautiful black fur, soft and warm against her fingers. The fire warmed her thin body and she relaxed for the first time. She began to think back to the weird happenings at the Assize Hall earlier…

She was convinced she had actually seen Matthew Weeks in the flesh. After all, she had met him once before with the striking young woman in the lane leading from Penhale Farm to the open moor. Yet the expression on his sullen face as he'd passed her on his way into the courtroom was one she would not forget. He looked haunted, and well he might be, if the stories were true about his brutal killing of the beautiful Charlotte Dymond.

Poppy did not feel in her heart that these tales rang true. There was something wrong with the way Matthew was being made into a scapegoat for the young woman's death. It seemed all too easy to put the blame on him. The croaky words of the obnoxious old man came back to her,

'We all do knaw Weeks is guilty!'

He had been gleeful, looking forward to a good hanging in the days ahead. But what could she do to help the condemned man?

'How ridiculous you are being,' she said out loud. 'Matthew Weeks has been dead for years. Since the year 1844 to be exact.'

She unwound her long legs and went over to the bookcase. Most of her own books were still packed in boxes at Josh's farmhouse, but she felt sure she had a couple of well-worn poetry books on the shelves. She picked out an anthology of Charles Causley's collected poems. She knew *The Ballad Of Charlotte Dymond* would be there. Clutching the book, Poppy resumed her warm place by the fire and flicked through the pages.

'Found it!'

Winston looked up at her nonchalantly from the rug. Poppy read the preface to the poem aloud:

Charlotte Dymond, a domestic servant aged eighteen, was murdered near Roughtor Ford on Bodmin Moor on Sunday 14 April 1844 by her young man: a crippled farm-hand, Matthew Weeks, aged twenty-two. A stone marks the spot.

She stared into the red caverns of the fire. The only sounds were the crackling and spitting of the twigs and Winston's rhythmic purring. She read the ballad right through to herself a couple of times, thinking of the curly-haired young man with the lop-sided grimace that she had seen at the Assize Court that morning. Somehow Poppy could not believe he murdered Charlotte, the pretty girl with the muddy petticoats that she had seen him with in the lane. She remembered Charlotte's enigmatic smile as she had turned to watch him limping along behind her. But she also remembered her hurtful words in the lane: 'I have to meet up with Tommy Prout later at the Chapel. I'm sorry Matthew... I don't want you. Go home.'

What if Charlotte had met someone else as she crossed the moor alone after leaving Matthew? Or had she met Tommy Prout as planned near the chapel? Was Tommy Prout just like a smiling Steve from Bodmin?

'There are daggers in men's smiles.' A few key words from *Macbeth* flashed into Poppy's head as she pulled the towel from her tangled red hair. She poured herself a large brandy. God only knows what Josh would think. Dear, kind Josh, who would do anything for her. She felt appalled at herself for letting herself be taken in by his so-called friend. Again she resolved that Josh must never know that Steve had tried to rape her. She sat by the fire, pensively stroking Winston's black fur. It was as black as the fast-approaching night.

Thirteen

TWO days later Josh arrived waving a letter in the air. Poppy peered out of the window at his weathered face, beaming at her. The latch rattled and there he was, obviously delighted about something.

He grabbed her in a bear-hug and then remembered it was not such a good idea. He flapped the paper above her head, grinning.

'Well? What's all the excitement about?'

Poppy could not help but smile. He was like a child.

'This came this morning! It was lost in the post. There's a reunion of our old year at school. Just think, it will be brilliant seeing all our old friends again.'

Poppy frowned.

'I'm not sure it's what I want at the moment, Josh.'

His smile faded.

'Oh come on, Poppy. It will be such a good laugh! You can't shut yourself away out here forever.'

She gazed out over the moorland and its tors. Somewhere out there a lone woman was walking... and she empathised with her solitary state.

'I just want to be left alone,' she sighed.

'Tough!'

Josh's face was full of anger.

'You're coming with me if I have to drag you all the way to Lanson.'

'Well when is this damned reunion anyway?' asked Poppy, turning to face him and speaking in a flat tone.

'On Saturday.'

Josh started to roll one of his strong cigarettes.

'Bloody hell,' Poppy said.

'You'll enjoy it when you get there,' Josh insisted.

'I doubt it very much,' she replied.

She put the kettle on and slung two tea-bags into mugs. Josh lit his cigarette. He dragged on it deeply as he watched her.

'Do you honestly think Matt would want you to be out here on your own all the time?'

He paused, smoke coming out of his nostrils.

'Of course he wouldn't! He would want you to carry on living. Carry on painting. Going out!'

'Don't bring Matt into this.'

Poppy poured milk into the mugs and spilled some on the work-top. She fished out the tea-bags and burst into tears.

'What a bloody mess!'

Josh wanted to comfort her, but instead he started to mop up the milk. Poppy sniffed into a ragged piece of tissue. Josh let her pull herself together for a bit, while he dragged for all he was worth on his cigarette. He ran a reddened hand through his hair. She walked to the window and, with her back to him, stared out at the line of moorland against the sky.

'I know you're right. I'm such a mess.'

She turned to him and with a supreme effort.

'But if you really want, yes I'll come to the damned reunion with you.'

Josh marvelled at Poppy's unexpected words.

'Thank Christ for that!'

He relaxed.

'You must start to live again. Even if it is only meeting up with a few prematurely balding blokes from school who used to lust after you in your uniform.'

'If that's supposed to make me feel better about going, then you have absolutely no idea, Josh.'

But she could see the expression of relief on his face now she had agreed. She had promised and would not go back on it. A couple of hours later she was in the fresh air, walking towards Crowdy Marsh. Josh had rattled off in his jeep, looking fairly satisfied with his persuasive techniques. Poppy's hands were thrust into her pockets as she walked down the track past an old stone barn, but her spirits lifted as she walked. She even began to sing under her breath, much to the surprise of the black cattle standing hock-deep in mud and filth. The path plunged towards the valley and the marshy ground surrounded her. She squelched through the mud and stopped to take her bearings.

'It's too boggy down there,' said a woman's voice.

Poppy looked around her. Instinct told her that the voice belonged to Charlotte Dymond. She was right, she was not alone any more, for there at the top of the bank was Charlotte, holding her skirts and petticoats up out of the mud.

'We could go back round the other way,' said a man's voice, which Poppy did not recognise. Further down the bank with a hand outstretched was the figure of a young man, laughing up into Charlotte's lovely face.

'Well I am not going to ruin my Sunday dress in the marshes, Tommy.'

Charlotte's voice faded as she turned away and started to clamber back up the slope.

'Wait for me! My best boots are full of bog-water,' pleaded the young man, his handsome features flushed with the effort of extricating himself from deep mud.

Poppy pulled her mobile out of her pocket and glanced at the time. It was just after three o'clock.

The man, Tommy, was following Charlotte up the slope. She was waiting at the top, weary and breathless. She watched the man ascending the slope towards her and the expression on her beautiful face changed to a smile.

'I bet she never looked at Matthew like that,' breathed Poppy.

'We could make our way up to the gate and on to Tremail, if you like,' Tommy panted, as he joined Charlotte at the top of the slippery bank.

He took her hand and she gave it. Her eyes sparkled as he brushed her face quickly with his lips. Then she pulled away.

'It is too early for the evening preaching at Tremail Chapel, Tommy.'

Charlotte adjusted her bonnet, which was askew.

'Let's get out of this boggy old ground and up into the lane.'

She picked up her skirts and petticoats and held them even higher, showing a pair of pretty ankles clad in black stockings. Tommy's eyes widened. He was captivated.

'What a waste it is to let that cripple, Matthew Weeks, look at your lovely long legs. I would appreciate them far more.'

He grinned knowingly while he spoke. Charlotte blushed deeply. She seemed momentarily at a loss for words faced with the confidence of Tommy Prout and his winning smile. Again he took her hand and together they turned their backs unconsciously on their spectator, and meandered up the lane. A whisper of moorland mist enveloped them...

Poppy's head was in a whirl. Was this, then, the young man who had met Charlotte after she left poor Matthew out on the moors after an argument? Could this handsome face have seduced Charlotte Dymond on an April afternoon all those years ago? One thing was for certain: Matthew, with his lop-sided smile and his gammy leg, had never caused Charlotte to blush and flirt like this. Poppy was certain of that. Yet her sense of time was all confused. For today Charlotte still seemed very much alive and in the flesh, so much so that Poppy felt she could have reached out to touch her.

Yet only a few days before she had seen poor Matthew at Bodmin's Assize Court, facing condemnation for her murder. As she squelched her way back to the cottage, Poppy's head was in a whirl. By the time she was putting her key in the lock her mind was made up. She would have to return to Bodmin. She needed to investigate more, visit the old gaol where Matthew had been incarcerated. She had not done so on her last visit because it had ended so disastrously. But now she felt determined to unravel more of the secrets from the past.

FOURTEEN

SATURDAY came, all too quickly. Sunlight washed the landscape and Poppy hung some washing out in the enclosed patch of garden. Sheep cropped the grass outside the stony wall and looked up with yellow eyes at the mangle's metallic squeak as she turned the huge handle.

'Why oh why did I promise to go to the reunion?' she muttered to herself as she cranked the handle furiously. 'And what on earth am I going to wear?'

A surreal vision of herself in tiara and wellies came out of her head.

'Don't be so silly!' Poppy yelled loudly at herself, scattering the startled sheep. 'Now I know I'm going mad, talking to myself while I peg the washing out. Thank God no one is around to hear me.'

She stooped to pick up the wicker flasket.

'I can hear you,' said a silvery voice.

Poppy spun around. There was nobody to be seen. Only the deserted lane, which led towards Penhale Farm. She had quite expected to see Charlotte Dymond there before her.

'Where are you?' she asked in a quavering voice.

The only answer was a sudden gust of wind and the flapping of her clothes on the washing-line. Poppy clutched the flasket tightly as she searched vainly for a glimpse of a human form nearby. Winston was staring at her, balefully, from the tiny window of the cottage. His glossy black fur shone with blue streaks in the sunlight.

'I was right,' she muttered, pushing open the cottage

door. 'Now I am beginning to imagine things, hear voices. I really must be going mad. I shall end up in St Lawrence's psychiatric hospital if I don't pull myself together.'

Once inside, she bolted the door. She moved to the window and stroked Winston, who was soon purring under her touch.

The garden and its environs were deserted as usual. Her bits of washing were blowing in the lively April breeze. Not a human in sight. Even the sheep had meandered away from the walls and were grazing rough pasture further away.

Poppy sighed and made herself a mug of strong tea. She trudged upstairs and pulled open the door of the small wardrobe.

Emptying two drawers on to the bed, she stared at her rumpled clothes. She sat down despairingly and lifted the mug from the chest of drawers. She sipped her tea.

'I must have a shower and wash my hair before I think of what to wear this evening,' she told herself. 'I don't even have a Little Black Dress for the occasion.'

A sudden flashback of Matt's funeral service hit her. She had not worn the expected black, preferring instead to wear a crinkled silk skirt he'd liked, in the colours of the sea. And a necklace of sea-green glass around her white throat that brought out the colour of her eyes. After all, she was his mermaid... had he not told her so at Zennor? Perhaps she could wear that to the reunion.

Six hours later, Josh arrived. He had scrubbed up well, Poppy thought as she peered out of the upstairs window. He looked handsome in a rugged sort of way.

She clattered down the stairs to open the door, wearing long leather boots that were already pinching her toes. Her red hair was freshly-washed and flowing free. The sea-green silk rippled around her booted calves. Her eyes glittered like the glass shards around her neck.

'Wow!'

Josh seemed amazed.

'You look fantastic, Poppy.'

'Well thank you, kind sir. It's only that you are so used to seeing me in baggy jeans and comfy clothes when I am here at home.'

'We'd better get going then,' said Josh jauntily, 'if we're to get to Eagle House on time.'

Poppy looked wistfully around the room thinking of how she wanted to stay cosily at home, instead of facing a lot of people from the past who would no doubt be nosing into her affair. The local newspaper had already covered the informative bits about Matt's suicide and inquest, but there are always unanswered questions. They drove up the lane and soon passed Davidstow Church. Poppy looked out of the jeep window at the churchyard bathed in the mellow light of early evening. Charlotte Dymond's body lay at rest there, she thought. But Poppy knew only too well that the poor girl's spirit was anything but resting…

Josh was thankfully quiet as he drove through the hamlet of Hallworthy. On her left was a small cottage, one of a row, originally a busy public house, The All Drunkards Inn. She had read that Matthew Weeks had been taken there from Plymouth after his arrest on the Hoe. This, then, was where the magistrates' hearing had taken place before he was committed to prison at Bodmin. Poppy shivered.

'Are you cold? There's an old jacket behind the seat if you need it,' said Josh, half-turning and starting to drag it forward. 'Mind you, it's probably covered in dogs' hair though.'

'No, I'm fine Josh. Honestly.'

Liar, she thought to herself. Soon she could see the white wind turbines at Cold Northcott creating their alien landscape. How she hated them. She remembered one beautiful day, riding a chestnut mare across the open heath where the turbines now stood. The sun was beating down and butterflies were flitting over the bright yellow gorse bushes. She imagined she could smell the coconut perfume of the gorse and the creak of the saddle leather beneath her.

'Were you listening to me?'

Josh's deep voice broke into her reverie.

'You were miles away.'

'Not miles away, actually. I was thinking of the times I used to go horse-riding at Laneast, that's all. Before all of these monsters spoiled the landscape.'

'Well, as I was saying, it should be a really good evening. It'll be great to see some of our old mates again.'

Poppy remained silent. She remembered some apt words from the beginning of a novel: *The past is a foreign country. They do things differently there.*

Where was it from? She racked her brains. The jeep was now approaching Tregadillett before joining the A30.

'That's it! *The Go-Between.*' she announced jubilantly.

'What the hell are you on about?'

Josh looked at her sideways, noting her flushed cheeks.

'I just remembered the title of a book. It's been bugging me, that's all.'

'That's half your trouble, Poppy. 'Too much reading and far too much imagination,'

Josh swerved to avoid a dead badger in the middle of the road. Poppy gripped the door handle.

'You can't ever have too much reading, Josh. You ought to try it sometime.'

'What, before I help on the farm? Or after rugby training?'

He glanced at her.

'Or perhaps you think I should take a good book with me when I'm out in the yard, building walls with father.'

They drove in silence for the remainder of the journey, each wrapped in their own thoughts. The jeep wound down past the walls of Launceston Castle. On their left were the old hunting grounds, known to locals as the Willow Gardens. Poppy could see the huntsmen quite clearly in her mind, galloping along the valley by the stream, chasing deer, arrows flying.

Perhaps Josh was right. She did have an over-ripe imagination. After all, there were only a few sheep and lambs on the steep slopes. Allotments were laid out below. Josh turned up Tower Street and grated the gears as he changed down to ascend the hill. Not long now, thought Poppy, before they turned right towards Eagle House Hotel and she would have to face school friends from her past. Her hands were sweating and her boots were killing her. She gritted her teeth as the jeep skidded on the gravel of the car park and stopped. Below the trees she could glimpse the beautiful white Georgian house, its lights twinkling as leaves moved in the cool breeze. It was time to face people from the past. But this time it was her own past which reared up before her, not that of Charlotte Dymond.

FIFTEEN

TOGETHER Poppy and Josh walked towards the gateposts topped by white stone eagles, wings outspread. The building was originally a private house, but had been a hotel for as long as she could remember. Poppy looked up at the outline of the roof, where Britannia stood proudly with her fishing prong. She was stunned to see the statue's robes painted a garish blue. No doubt John Betjeman would have been equally mortified at the change, she thought, having described this street with its Georgian houses as *'one of the most beautiful in England'*.

Josh led the way and Poppy trailed unhappily in his wake, her heart thumping away. It was hot in the reception area. She looked about at the familiar flight of stairs and a ornate couch, upholstered in a deep rose fabric. Poppy desperately wanted to sit on the couch and put off the awful moment of descending the staircase to enter the ballroom. She could imagine facing an upturned sea of faces. She glanced at Josh, who was already talking in an animated fashion to some unrecognisable person on the top step. Poppy forced herself to walk towards them and fixed a smile on her face. The man turned towards her.

'I was sorry to hear about your fiance,' he said gently.

Her fiance. Is that what Matt was?

Josh smiled encouragingly at her.

'You remember Rob, don't you? He was in the year above us, doing sciences.'

'Of course I do,' she lied. 'Thanks Rob.'

She looked into the stranger's face and thought that maybe there was something about his sympathetic grey eyes that she remembered.

'I would have sent a card but I had no idea where you lived nowadays.'

Rob shifted uncomfortably.

'It's fine. Don't apologise. Really.'

Was the whole evening going to be like this, with people walking on egg-shells around her?

'Come on then, let's get to the bar.'

Josh grabbed her arm impulsively and they left Rob staring down at them from the top of the stairs. A hubbub of noise came from behind the double doors.

'This is it then. Just hold your head up and try to relax a bit.'

Josh pushed the door open and the heat and noise hit them. She was aware of a packed room and loud music as they fought their way to the bar. A hand touched her back and she turned to face Aid. They had been great friends at school. His face had lost its youthful, Adonis look and his blonde hair was touched with silvering streaks. He was different and no doubt he was thinking that about her, too.

'Hi Poppy. Good to see you.'

He kissed her lightly on her cheek.

'You look great.'

'You too, Aid.'

She remembered the way he flicked his floppy hair back.

'Have you seen any of our old gang?' Aid asked.

Poppy shook her head.

'Not yet. But then we've only just arrived.'

Josh passed her a glass of red wine. He was deep in conversation with two girls. She sipped her wine nervously.

'Not drinking Pernod any more then?' Aid smiled, thinking of past parties and binges.

'No. Not any more,' Poppy said quietly.

'Do you remember the time we had a sixth form party at my place, when my parents were away?'

Poppy laughed. Who could forget the loud music and chaos? She could even taste Pernod for what had seemed like weeks afterwards.

'We had some brilliant times, didn't we?'

Aid gulped down the remainder of his beer and motioned to Poppy's wine glass.

'No,' she said, putting her hand over her glass. 'I'm okay for a bit, thanks.'

Aid flicked his hair back again with that well-remembered movement.

'I'll just get another pint. Don't go away.'

He was quickly lost in the crowd. Poppy looked around for Josh but he was nowhere to be seen. She noticed a display of old school photos on the wall. A gaggle of girls surrounded it, pointing and shrieking at the images. She made her way towards the display and put on her interested, 'cheerful' face.

'Poppy!'

Another shriek.

'How lovely to see you!'

One of the group rushed over and embraced her. Others followed, one or two with uncomfortable glances. Soon she was surrounded by old friends and former classmates. At first there was lots of superficial chat.

'Your hair is still amazing,' said Annie's familiar voice. 'The red catches the light. I remember when it was so long that you could sit on it when I drew you in art lessons.'

'I can't do that any more.'

Poppy fingered the strands of her hair.

'But you still look just like a pre-Raphaelite painting.'

Annie smiled at her and squeezed her arm gently. Poppy sucked in her breath. Pre-Raphaelite. Matt's description of her. Annie saw the tears there and drew her to one side.

'Do you want to sit outside for a while? It's really hot in here.'

Poppy nodded. They struggled through the crowd with their wine glasses. The doors were open on to a patio with tables and benches and they chose a dark corner under the moving leaves.

'Tell me what really happened, Poppy,' Annie said gently.

It was almost a relief to talk about it after the months of anguish and sleepless nights. The feelings of guilt, the remorse, the sense of loss. Time passed in the talk of close friends. Josh came looking for Poppy, his face showing his relief to see her. The girls' intimacy was broken as he chatted to Annie about schooldays.

'Did you know that Chris is gay now? I can't bloody believe it.'

He swilled back his beer, shaking his head.

'And Dave is getting married to Kate! Her marriage only lasted a few months and they met up again through *Friends Reunited*.'

Poppy and Annie smiled at each other as Josh continued relentlessly,

'And Joe would have been here tonight but Maggie's about to give birth.'

Annie cut him off.

'That'll do Josh! It's too much to take in at one go.'

She stood up.

'Let's go in and get some more drinks. Coming Poppy?'

'No, I'll just sit here for a bit longer and smoke a cigarette,' said Poppy. 'You go on in. I'll be fine.'

She took a sip of wine. A deep voice made her start. It was a voice she knew well. Her stomach churned.

'I thought you must be hiding away somewhere.'

'I didn't realise you were here,' she said quietly, blowing cigarette smoke into the dark corner. Simon slumped down opposite her. He looked wasted. His eyes were bloodshot. She remembered how possessive he used to be when he'd had a few drinks.

'And how is the most beautiful girl in our year? On her own, I see. Well that makes a change.'

Simon's voice was slurred. He leaned over the table and reached for her thin white hand, which was holding the stem of her glass. Too late she pulled her hand back and the dregs of wine spilled She picked up the glass quickly as it rolled towards the edge of the table.

'Sorry. I only wanted to hold your hand Poppy.'

He grinned.

'We're old friends, after all.'

She remembered Simon's wet, drunken kisses. His jealousy. The terrible rows when they were nineteen years old.

'It was nearly empty Simon, don't worry.'

'I'll get you another drink.'

He lurched to his feet.

'No thanks.'

'That was always the bloody trouble with you Poppy, you were so damned offish.'

Simon's spit shot out of his contorted mouth.

'Unless there was someone else hanging around for you to flirt with of course, just to make me jealous.'

Flushed, she opened her mouth to respond, but suddenly she forgot the present.

She could hear another voice saying: 'It was

disgraceful of you, meeting up with Tommy Prout before chapel.'

And there, quite clearly in front of her, in place of Simon, was the face of Matthew Weeks.

SIXTEEN

EAGLE House's bright lights and loud music had disappeared. Matthew Weeks stood in a muddy Cornish lane and Poppy could hear the plaintive bleating of young lambs on the other side of a hedge, where yellow gorse bloomed. He appeared to be talking to a man, who was leaning on a shovel and had his back to her. Matthew's expression was sullen and dogged as he muttered.

'It's that Tommy Prout that I'd like to have words with, he won't leave Charlotte alone. And there's days when she even seems to encourage him, just to make me jealous.'

'Well Matthee, remember that time out in the mowhay soon after Lady Day? Tommy said that he was thinking to come to live at Penhale,' replied the man.

He continued in a teasing voice.

'It do seem to me like he's some sweet on your Charlotte himself, for didn't he say he'd deprive you of your girlfriend afore too long?'

Matthew flushed red with anger.

'Well if 'e moves into Penhale, then I'll be moving out John, and that's a promise. 'Tis bad enough having quarrelled about them bullocks with his miserable uncle, Isaac Cory, without having to see that cocksure Tommy grinning across the table in the farmhouse every day.'

'Don't take on so, Matthee, 'twill all come out in the wash.'

Shouldering his muddy shovel, John plodded off up the lane, shaking his head and leaving Matthew standing alone with a face like thunder, unaware that Poppy was standing beside him. He started to follow John up the lane, moodily kicking at clods of drier mud. His face betrayed his feelings of anger and imminent loss.

Poppy broke into a profuse sweat. The gorse bushes and the country lane vanished. It was the first time she had regressed when she was away from Penhale and the surrounding moorland. One minute she had been talking to a rather drunken Simon in the garden of Eagle House in Launceston, the next she had been in a lane listening to a brief snatch of conversation between Matthew Weeks and a man called John, who seemed to have worked with him on the farm near Davidstow. Suddenly she vomited violently with no warning, and swivelled to face the dark gardens. Her head was banging painfully and the sour stench of sick was on her hands and clothes.

'Too much to drink eh?'

Simon's slurring voice reached her from the doorway.

'You never could hold your booze, Poppy.'

'Leave her alone, Simon. It's bloody obvious she's not well.'

Josh pushed past him angrily. Poppy sat down weakly on a wooden bench.

'Where did Matthew go?' she asked, confused.

'Who the hell is Matthew?'

Simon leered at her.

'Told you you were pissed.'

Josh pushed him away aggressively,

'And I told you to leave Poppy alone. If anyone's drunk, it's you!'

'I want to go home Josh... can you get me a taxi? I don't want to spoil your evening.'

She was beginning to pull herself together.

'I shouldn't have come.'

Josh looked at Poppy and sighed. She looked a mess. The sea-green silk skirt was spattered with sick and she was deathly-pale.

'It doesn't matter. I'll take you home,' he said in a resigned tone.

Simon looked at them talking to each other for a long moment. There was an indecipherable expression in his bleary eyes, then without another word he lurched back into the party, clutching an empty pint glass, in search of the bar.

Josh was true to his word. Despite being stupidly over the limit, he drove her home. There was little conversation between them because she was slumped against the window of the jeep with her eyes closed. Waves of nausea flowed over her as the jeep bumped its way along the lane leading to the cottage. There was almost a full moon silvering the landscape. The moor bathed tranquilly in its light.

She got out of the jeep with some difficulty. Josh supported her as she staggered to the cottage door. She certainly seemed a bit drunk, Josh thought. Poppy put her key in the lock mechanically. Once inside, she collapsed on to the sofa and closed her eyes painfully.

'You're shaking like a leaf,' Josh said. 'Time for you to go to bed I reckon. You look like you could do with a good kip.'

Poppy opened her eyes slowly,

'I'm so sorry, Josh. I've messed up your evening and I know how much you were looking forward to it.'

He bent down to her on the sofa and spoke softly.

'What the hell did you mean when you asked where Matthew had gone? He's gone Poppy. He's dead.'

Josh stood up and his knees clicked painfully.

'I know it's hard, but you've got to start coming to terms with the fact that he's not coming back.'

'Not my Matthew, the other one. Matthew Weeks. He was talking to me at Eagle House,' she answered wearily.

Josh looked stunned.

'Who?'

He grabbed her thin arms roughly and shook her.

'You've got to stop all this load of bollocks! Matthew Weeks? You mean the bloke who killed Charlotte Dymond? Well he's dead too. He's been dead for bloody ages, you know that!'

He was shouting now.

'My gran even told you how he was hanged at Bodmin Gaol. You've got to get a grip on reality and stop imagining these crazy things all the time... or you'll end up in Bodmin psychiatric hospital yourself.'

She hung limply in his arms, like a rag doll, feeling totally disorientated, and waited for the swirling motion to pass.

'You look bloody awful, Poppy.'

He was calmer now that he could see what a state she was in.

'I'm going to get you up the stairs to bed, but you'll have to help me a bit.'

Josh supported her and somehow they struggled up the narrow stairs to the bedroom. She sat on the edge of the rumpled bed with its discarded clothes and Josh pulled off her leather boots with difficulty. He peeled her silk skirt and top off and dropped them on the floor. Both stank of her sick. She shivered uncontrollably. He bundled her into bed, scattering her crumpled clothes, and tucked the duvet around her.

'Better?' he asked; his voice had lost its harsh tone.

She nodded, eyes closed.

'Do you still feel sick?'

She shook her head on the pillow.

'I'll be downstairs if you need me. Just shout.'

Josh took a last despairing look at her before descending the stairs. The cottage was silent. Silver light streaked through the window. Josh looked out at the sleeping moorland. It all looked so still, so tranquil in the moonlight. Yet it had not brought tranquillity to Poppy, that was for sure. Her behaviour seemed more and more deranged. He lit the brass lamp and then wrenched the curtains across.

'Bloody place! I knew she shouldn't have come out here to live.' he muttered.

Winston padded towards him, his tail in the air like a question mark. He rubbed against Josh's legs. Well at least the bloody cat was getting used to him being around, he thought savagely. Josh searched for a drink and found two more empty brandy bottles hidden behind the curtain under the sink. Luckily there was some left in a third bottle. He sloshed some into a glass and drank and sat down heavily on the sofa to roll an untidy cigarette, which he lit and inhaled deeply.

What a fricking disaster the evening had turned out to be. He thought back to the good time he'd been having earlier in the company of old mates. Why did Poppy always spoil everything for him? He took another slug of brandy. The hard truth stared him in the face. It was no good trying to blame her for everything. He loved her, despite all her weird ways – but wherever Poppy looked, there were ghosts. If it wasn't Matt's, then it was Charlotte Dymond's... and now even the ghost of her murderer was wafting around. He drained the bottle. One thing he was sure of, she needed him. She was a right bloody mess and it was up to him to get her through it.

Josh sighed and stubbed out his cigarette. He dragged a heavy throw over himself and curled up for an unsettled night's sleep, Winston purring loudly beside him.

Seventeen

JOSH left a scribbled note the next morning. He had gone to work, driving through the morning mist to St Clether. The sun was breaking through the clouds when Poppy finally awoke. She had been dreaming of being back at Morwenstow and the waves were crashing below the cliffs. Matt was standing on the cliff-edge looking down at the razor-sharp rocks below. She could not reach him, and she heard her voice shouting hoarsely 'Nooooo...' but drowned by the calls of the seabirds. He turned to look at her with a strange smile. She could see his face at last. Then she saw him go over...

Wiping the sweat away, Poppy crawled out of bed. She felt desperately tired and tearful. Somehow she had to put those horrific images of Matt's death out of her mind. Showered and feeling better, wrapped in a soft scarlet jumper and clean jeans, she made a cup of milky coffee and drank it while she looked out of the window. The tors looked distant today, partly hidden by mist.

An hour later she was driving on the open moor past St Breward towards Delphi Bridge. She pulled in by the river and watched two donkeys grazing peacefully near the water. The wind was blowing gently and she could hear the distant drone of a light aircraft somewhere up in the blue. It was incredibly beautiful there by the stream. The water slid over huge stones and a small beach of gravel had formed near the bridge. It was pitted with the tracks of cattle and ponies. A small bird of prey, probably a kestrel with its distinctive pointed wings and long tail, hovered high above. Poppy rolled a cigarette and surveyed the landscape. In just such a lonely place Charlotte Dymond had met her violent death. She lit the cigarette and inhaled deeply. The donkeys had moved away. Poppy stuck the cigarette in her mouth and switched on the ignition. The larger donkey looked up mildly before dropping his head to the turf once more. The car crunched on the gravel as it pulled away from the stream-side and on to the single track road. A mile or so further on, she was stubbing her cigarette out when an ancient tractor appeared alarmingly around a hidden bend. A red-faced farmer yelled: 'Get out the bleddy way, maid!'

Poppy slammed on the brakes and her car scraped a stony hedge. She was dazed. In front of her was a sign-post at the cross-roads. Blisland.

'Tell Matthew that I have gone to Blisland.'

She remembered the white face of a woman at her window on the night of her terror. It was as if Charlotte Dymond had been trying to tell her something that night. Something that might have given her a clue about what really happened all those years ago. The farmer and tractor had vanished and she sat in the car, motionless. Above her she could hear a skylark trilling and the sun was breaking through the clouds. Before her was the sign-post pointing its wooden finger towards Blisland.

Poppy started the engine and manoeuvred the car away from the hedge with a metallic screech. In a dream-like state she drove down the road away from the open moor towards wooded valleys. Below was Blisland village with its granite cottages and houses clustered round the village green. She pulled in by the church gate and sat with her eyes closed. Rooks were cawing somewhere in the vicinity of the lichened church tower.

'It's no good you just sitting there with your eyes closed,' said a woman's voice, sharply.

Poppy sat up and opened her eyes. The woman, of about sixty or so with a weathered face and clothed in black with a spotless white apron, was standing in a substantial, old-fashioned kitchen. She was talking to a man sitting sullenly in a window seat, his head bowed.

'Matthee! There's a lot of bad talk about you and Charlotte. The neighbours be all talking about it. That maid's been missing for some days now and you walked out together. All that talk about her leaving Penhale, well I don't believe a word of it.'

The man got up and went over to the far side of the kitchen. He turned to face her, an obstinate expression on his face.

''T'is true mistress! Charlotte said she were going over to Blisland to service. She said she'd found an easier place to work.'

Poppy could see from the woman's tightly-pursed lips and the expression in her dark, slitted eyes that she was having none of it. Matthew Weeks, for she could see clearly now that it was him, was speaking defensively.

'To tell the truth, t'was your niece Rebecca who told her 'bout the place in Blisland parish.'

The shrewd-eyed woman shook her head in obvious disbelief.

'Charlotte told me when we were out doing the milking that you had given her a week's notice.'

There was a stunned silence at this somewhat confrontational remark. The woman looked a little confused, then replied with more authority.

'I would never give notice on a Sunday, Matthew. You d'know that. And how could Charlotte walk out to Blisland on a Sunday night when t'would be getting dark afore too long?'

'The maid even asked to borrow some money from me afore she went. She said she was going to walk on to

Brown Willy after her left me, to stay at Hezekiah Spear's cottage that night; then on to Blisland the next day.'

Matthew spoke in earnest to his employer now. He took a deep breath and continued with more conviction now.

'Mistress, why don't you ask Tom Prout or his brother whether they'd seed her on the moor?'

Matthew's mouth twisted with hatred at the mere mention of the Prout boys.

'Tommy Prout paid her a visit here last Sunday morning as you d'know. He was sitting there on the settle by the fire.'

He pointed to the settle of dark wood

'Afore they went outside to talk in the yard.'

'I d'remember Thomas being here for a while.'

Her brows knitted as she thought hard.

'But Charlotte still walked out with you in the afternoon, Matthew, up the lane in the direction of Higher Down Gate.'

The outside door opened and their talk was interrupted. A man stooped as he entered from the porch. Poppy recognised him as the man with the muddy shovel in the lane with Matthew who'd been teasing him about Tommy being sweet on his Charlotte.

'Where have you been John?'

The woman's voice was imperious now.

'You should have finished the yard work some time afore this.'

'Sorry mistress, I was mucking out, same as usual, but there was some bother with the stable door. The bolt needed some fixing. Proper rusty t'were.'

He went to the stone sink and began washing his filthy hands. He looked back over his left shoulder at Matthew.

'Charlotte is not come back yet then, Matthee? Where is that maid gone to?'

'I don't know,' said Matthew. 'I only wish I did know. T'would stop all of you keepin' on at me. Seems to me you folk have little faith in me.'

He turned and went on up the stairs heavily without another word to either of them. John, shrugged and went back to scrubbing his hands and arms at the sink. The farm's mistress continued to stare long and hard at the now empty staircase, where Matthew had stood only moments before...

'Are you all right?' asked a gentle voice.

Poppy started. She was still sitting in her car by the church gate. An elderly man in a dog-collar was staring down into her car at her. A faded cassock was folded over his arm.

'Yes... I'm fine, thanks,' she stuttered.

'You have been sitting there in your car for over an hour. I noticed you looked rather strange, your eyes were staring straight ahead. For a minute I thought you might have been taken ill.'

'No, I think I must have drifted off to sleep,' Poppy said rather weakly. 'I'm on my way to Bodmin. I have secrets to unearth there.'

She was aware of the man's look of concern and pulled herself together.

'Thanks anyway.'

She started her car up with a burst of blue exhaust smoke. The kindly vicar stood back and she gave him a quick wave, before driving quickly away from the village green, towards the main road to Bodmin.

Half an hour later Poppy pulled in below the high, grim walls of the ruinous gaol, set in a valley next to the old railway track.

EIGHTEEN

THE walls of the former county prison were dizzyingly high as she looked up at them. 'Nobody could ever climb over that lot,' she thought as she parked her car and walked around the corner to the gaol's main gate. 'No wonder they kept the Crown Jewels and the Doomsday Book here during the First World War. You'd have to be mad to even attempt those walls.'

Poppy stood in front of the huge, imposing gateway. On her left were two tall, dour-looking granite houses: one was still named The Chaplaincy, the other was the former residence of the prison's governor. How must Matthew Weeks have felt as, escorted by constables, he was driven in a cart under the gloomy portal? Had he known then in his heart that he would end his earthly days in this grim building with its row upon row of tiny cell windows? She shivered. What did she hope to achieve in this ghastly place?

'Someone has just walked over my grave,' she said softly to herself, 'Or perhaps I am about to walk over someone else's grave.'

Poppy knew that all those hanged there would have been buried in the prison precincts.

'No decent burial and headstone for them,' she said aloud.

She remembered that her father had told her the gaol had been a nightclub in the 1970s. Strange to think of it now. Music, laughter, dancing and gambling, all carrying on in the prison chapel with its stained glass windows, in the very same building that once housed desperate prisoners. Many of the original inmates, men and women, would have been doing 'hard labour' under the stony gaze of warders. Even young children were taken there to be flogged.

'Did you want to look inside?' asked a man's voice behind her.

Poppy swivelled around. His appearance was unexpected. He was stocky and muscular, dressed in a black t-shirt sporting a Bodmin Gaol logo. He was carrying a crate of empty beer bottles, which he dumped, the bottles clinking, with other crates inside the gateway. He rubbed his meaty red hands, which were tattooed with 'Love' and 'Hate' on the knuckles.

'The bar's open, if you fancy a drink. And we have a restaurant too, recently refurbished.'

'Thanks, but I'm not hungry,' Poppy replied. 'But perhaps I'll have a drink.'

She followed him to an open courtyard. It was empty. Poppy sat down nervously at a table. She had felt strange since entering the confines of the last gaol in Cornwall. A black-edged sign advertised 'Execution Shed'. A noose dangled ominously above an open pit. She felt sick.

The man vanished up steps towards the bar, away from the place of execution. She found him resting his huge muscular arms on the bar. He grinned at her.

'What do you fancy then?'

'Not you that's for sure,' she said to herself.

'Got a nice drink called Gaolbreak. You ought to try it. Most people think it's awesome.'

He grinned again, exposing a glinting gold tooth.

'I don't think so. I'll have a lager please.'

She forced a smile and fumbled for her purse. The kitchen door opened. There was a quick blast of radio punctuated by the sound of clattering pots and pans.

86

'Up to you, sweetheart.'

The man started to pour her drink.

'And I'm not your bloody sweetheart either,' she thought, furiously.

The lager was passed across the bar. Her money was paid into the outstretched 'Hate' hand. How appropriate, she mused, sipping lager. The man closed the till with a flourish.

'Would you like to see the list of executions?'

He made it sound like a menu. Poppy shivered. A sudden chilly wind blew through the room from a maze of twisting passages and dark cells.

'About fifty-five hangings took place around here, you know.'

The man's coarse voice faded into the background.

It was cold. The walls ran with water. A small barred window let in the grey light. The door grated open and two dour-looking turnkeys attempted to carry the limp body of a man into the cell.

'Put 'en down on the pallet. He's in a faint, 'tis all.'

The man's body slithered to the straw pallet on the dank floor.

'Weeks! Wake up!'

The shorter turnkey kicked the man's body viciously.

'You'm back in your cell.'

Matthew Weeks slowly opened his eyes and blinked. The bars of the cell window were silhouetted, high above him. A distant bird flew across the square of light.

'Wish I were as free as that bird,' he said in a low voice.

'Then you shouldn't 'ave killed that there pretty maid.'

The sneering tones of the taller turnkey rang loudly around the desolate cell, as he put a huge iron key in the lock. The beefier warder nodded in silent agreement.

'You'd best make your peace with the Lord now, Weeks. What was it that there Judge said when he sentenced you today?'

'You shall be taken hence to the place from whence you came and be hung by the neck until you are dead!'

The beefier warder relished reciting the words.

'Well you'll be as free as that there bird afore too long.'

The final jeering words and subsequent laughter accompanied the clanging to of the heavy cell door.

Poppy turned her attention to the condemned man before her. Matthew Weeks lay prostrate on his pallet, in a state of shock. His eyes were staring up, unseeing, at the tiny gap of sky. His pock-marked face was as pale as death. The row of glass buttons on his blue cloth jacket, which was crumpled from a long day at the Assize Court, winked in the slanting beams of light from the barred window. The light in the tiny cell started to fade. Matthew still lay, seemingly lifeless, on his narrow bed. Then words came.

'But I didn't kill Charlotte. I didn't.'

His eyes filled suddenly with unmanly tears. He whispered to himself: 'I loved that maid more'n life itself.'

And then he rolled slowly over on to his side and turned his face to the cold, wall.

Poppy reached out to touch the wretched man's shoulder in an instinctive act of human kindness. Instead of flesh and blood, Poppy found herself smoothing the coarse grey jacket of a life-like effigy.

'Quite real isn't it?'

A woman's voice at her side made Poppy reel in shock. She was standing in a cell similar to that occupied by Matthew Weeks. A small girl, clutching the woman's hand, was staring up at her.

Poppy realised her own face was wet with tears. She wiped it with her sleeve. Her heart was beating so loudly she was sure the woman must be able to hear it. The woman continued speaking.

'I'm beginning to think I shouldn't have brought my daughter in here. It's so grim, isn't it.'

'Well it *is* an old gaol,' Poppy muttered under her breath.

The little girl, who seemed totally unmoved by her surroundings, stared at Poppy without blinking.

'But then, it's so important for the young to experience some real-life history, don't you think?'

The mother looked around the desolate cell with a sense of satisfaction.

'So many children only visit theme parks nowadays.'

Poppy began to make her way down the stone steps. Her legs felt weak and she was still in a state of some confusion. She could sense ghosts in the atmosphere around her, here in this terrible place. The air crackled with them. She could hear the voices of long-dead men and women whispering. And the whispering and sighing grew louder and louder with each step she took. Many had died by the rope, and now they came towards her, their poor twisted necks marked with purple bruising like ripe blackberry stains, their hands outstretched. She could even smell them, in their grave clothes, in the shadows. Momentarily she felt paralysed, and then she stumbled blindly towards the gaol's open gateway, away from the clinging dead, away from the past and out into the road and the real world.

She sat in her car, shaking. Her mobile phone started ringing.

Nineteen

ANNIE'S name came up on her mobile as it rang and then rang again. Poppy sighed and put the phone back into her bag. Her hands were still shaking after her experience inside the gaol. She could not even bear to think of talking to Annie, who would be sympathetic and make her hate herself more than she did already. She would phone her later. Maybe.

She started up the car and turned her back on the road to the moors. She needed to go somewhere to smell the sea and watch the waves. She needed to think. Her mind was full of people and happenings.

It was late afternoon when she reached Polzeath. Its familiar beach was almost deserted, apart from a distant dog-walker on the tideline. Poppy parked her car on the top of the cliffs at New Polzeath and opened the window. The wind blew in gustily with the sea on its breath. She breathed in deeply. If only it could blow away the tangled cobwebs of her mind. The white horses of the waves stampeded towards the shore and smashed on to the slate-grey cliffs. There was a roar as Atlantic rollers moved majestically towards the empty beach. Strangely there were no surfers out.

Poppy climbed out of the car and pulled on a fleece. The air was salty on her lips. She felt elated. She started down the narrow cliff path that she had walked as a child with her father. A gull hung in the air high above her. Tamarisk and tough grass were flattened in the strong breeze. Sand blew up, stinging her eyes. Her long red hair whipped her face, yet she felt more alive than she had done for months. Her senses were sharpened. She tramped along the path and realised with some surprise that she was feeling hungry. She had not eaten at the gaol in Bodmin, but now the salty air made her suddenly ravenous. The beach cafe had closed early because there were very few visitors around, only an elderly couple rumped up in their car and pouring hot tea from a Thermos flask. The path started to flatten out as it wound behind the shelter of a hawthorn hedge and the roar of the surf was quieter. A flashback from her childhood holidays revealed the Treasure House, as it had then been called. It had been a children's paradise, full of sparkling trinkets and toys. Now it appeared to be yet another freshly-painted B&B, ready and waiting for the holiday season.

Poppy walked towards the main thoroughfare of Polzeath. Before long it would be packed with people, the pavements outside shops would be a clutter of bright buckets and spades, fishing nets, surf boards, wetsuits, and racks of postcards.

But it was only April and still quiet, a chilly breeze blowing in from the sea. She found a tiny cafe open and after a cup of tea and a toasted tea-cake, she made her way back up the cliff path, puffing and blowing. Below her the waves surged in towards the cliffs, sending spray high into the air. Matt had loved wave-watching, she thought, and suddenly she was back at Morwenstow looking down at his body on the razor-sharp reef below. Huge wracking sobs suddenly shook her body. The pain in her chest was unbearable. It was as if she had lost him all over again.

The sea darkened and there was a sense of desolation over the landscape. Out there were fathoms of cold, cold water and above the seagulls cried mournfully in the grey sky. Poppy looked up at the gulls and remembered the haunting words of Gweniver, Josh's granny, a seaman's widow.

'Each gull is the soul of a drowned sailor.'

Gweniver would not behave in such a pathetic manner, weeping on the cliffs, thought Poppy. Oh no, she would be strong. She would be baking and scrubbing, keeping herself busy, making sure her quaint little Boscastle cottage with its Gothic windows was as neat as a new pin.

A gleam of sunshine broke suddenly from behind the grey cloud and its slanting rays bathed the cliff-top in warmth and light. Poppy pulled herself together and wiped her eyes. All around was the wild beauty of nature, so much that it caught the back of her throat. The powerful waves rolled in as they had ever done. The dry sand blew up from the path into her eyes. The brittle grasses rustled as they moved in the wind. Nothing had changed, yet it seemed to her that everything in her life had. She pulled her fleece more tightly to her body and stumbled to the car. She sat there for a while, the wind buffeting the car, aware of the fading light. A sea mist was starting to drift in towards the coastline. She needed to get back to her homely cottage, with its firelight and cosy lamps.

She started the engine and switched on the radio. She was drowned in the rasping voice of Bob Dylan. Against her will it made her see Matt again, strumming his guitar in St Ives. The weather was hot. She could smell the salt and coconut oil in the air. Summer crowds pushed and jostled. A boat with a green sail could be seen in the distance, like one of the many primitive seascapes Alfred Wallis painted on scraps of cardboard. Matt's wonderful eyes met hers, his tanned hands fingering the guitar strings. Cool white cotton sheets. Their bodies interlocking in the darkness. Tangled hair, damp from love-making…

'Lay lady lay, lay across my big brass bed... His clothes are dirty but his hands are clean... And you're the best thing that he's ever seen... Lay lady lay, lay across my big brass bed...'

She turned down the sound and swung the car away from the cliffs and the thunder of the waves below.

Twenty

THE knocking at the door woke Poppy, who was in the middle of a strange dream, floating in restless seas with her father. He was smiling at her, as she clung to his old wooden surfboard. A wave took him away from her and she was shouting for him above the roar of the surf.

Again the knocking. Louder this time, insistent. She dragged herself out of bed. Whoever it was knocking would not give up. She pulled on her dressing-gown and started groggily down the stairs, nearly tripping over Winston in the shadows. The cottage smelled stale, with the added tang of cat's pee.

'Poppy? Open this bloody door.'

Bang!

'It's Annie!'

Bang! bang! More thumps on the cottage door. Wearily, Poppy unbolted the door and Annie pushed it open. A clean blast of fresh air came in off the moor with her.

'God it stinks in here,' she said, wrinkling her nose with distaste. Poppy shut the door, irritated by the intrusion.

'Thanks a lot.'

'What the hell is going on with you, Poppy?' Annie said angrily, eyes blazing. 'I've been trying and trying to ring you since you were ill at the reunion. But you won't answer. You're like a bloody recluse.'

Poppy faced her best friend from school.

'Oh Annie, I just want to be left alone that's all. I don't feel like socialising. It's not a crime.'

She pulled back the curtains over the stone sink and started to fill the kettle.

'It's not doing you any good, Poppy. What you need is company and a few laughs. Perhaps a girls' night out in a pub with some good food and music.'

Annie put her arm around Poppy's thin shoulders, shocked at her bones sticking out.

'I'm fine, stop fussing over me like a mother hen. Look I'll just go and get dressed, you can make the tea.'

Annie watched her friend climb the stairs slowly. She turned to the window. The pale light filtered through the panes on to her fair hair, caught back in a heavy, untidy plait. Her jumble of bright, unusual clothes, thrown together haphazardly, made a vivid splash of colour. Her dark eyes searched the landscape outside. Nothing but strange-shaped stones, heather and bloody sheep. No wonder Poppy was going stir-crazy. She had imprisoned herself out here in a granite cell and put the barricades up to the whole world. Well enough was enough. Even Josh was at his wit's end, it seemed, judging from his conversation on the phone last night.

'I can't get her to do anything Annie,' he'd sighed. 'She's determined to keep herself to herself with her memories of Matt. Look what happened at Eagle House. She couldn't cope with all those people. She's not eating and she's drinking far too much. Take a look at the empties under the sink if you don't believe me. Perhaps you could go out and try and talk to her. She might listen to you.'

'I wouldn't bank on it,' she'd muttered.

He had hesitated.

'But that's not all. She's obsessed with some girl who was killed years ago at Roughtor. Says she keeps on seeing her out on the moors. And some weird bloke called Matthew.'

Poor besotted Josh, he'd seemed really desperate, pleading with her on the end of the phone. Annie knew she had a couple of days off, so she'd headed out towards Davidstow to find out for herself what was really happening at Penhale Cottage.

She bent down and peered behind the curtain under the sink. Several empty wine bottles and at least three brandy bottles stood next to a packet of washing powder and a bottle of bleach. Guiltily she pulled the curtain across, glanced at the stairs and stood up quickly to make the tea. Spying on her friend was not something Annie felt proud of, especially as her own garage was overflowing with empty wine bottles.

Winston slunk out of a dark corner and yowled for food. He even rubbed his glossy black body against her boots. By the time Poppy was downstairs again, the cat had been fed, the tea was rapidly cooling and Annie had obviously sprayed her very expensive perfume around the room to eliminate the essence of cat's pee.

'Let's go out somewhere. Do a bit of retail therapy, Poppy. It'll be just like old times.'

Annie's voice was artificially bright and breezy.

'We can ransack the charity shops and have lunch somewhere.'

Poppy grimaced into her mug of tea and put it down distastefully by the sink.

'Is there any point in my saying I really don't want to go shopping, of all things?'

'Absolutely not.'

Annie suddenly sounded like a brisk hospital matron, as she too put her cup by the sink.

'Come on Poppy, it'll do you good to get out of this bloody awful place for a few hours. You might as well be in a prison cell doing solitary.'

Poppy closed her eyes at Annie's words. When she

opened them again, the curtains at the window had disappeared. Iron bars had taken their place. Shafts of watery light poured in on her. The walls of her cottage had mysteriously closed in. Gone were her vivid paintings with their daubs of primary colour. A terrible greyness had closed over everything. A pile of rags lay on the damp stone floor. The only sounds were the drip, drip of rain from the cell window high above and distant echoes of heavy doors slamming shut. For some minutes she stood there, taking in the scene. She had been here before. She was back inside the miserable confines of Bodmin Gaol. She could hear the far-off shrieks of women and the deeper voices of men. The stench in the cell was unbearable. The huge pile of what seemed like rags began to stir. Under it was a human being, looking up at the barred window with empty, staring eyes.

Matthew Weeks looked gaunt and pale in the morning light. Months in prison awaiting his trial had taken away a healthy, weathered look gained from a life spent tending livestock in the open air on the farm. As he stood up, with apparent difficulty, she saw clearly his shrunken muscles and the grey-white pallor of his skin. He looked a dead man already. The sound of a heavy key rattled in the lock and the cell door scraped open. She recognised the beefy, red-faced turnkey as he ushered in a thin man wearing clerical dress, the prison chaplain.

'Here's the condemned man, Mr Kendall sir. Name of Weeks. Hope you can stand the terrible stink in here whilst you talk to him.'

Beefy red-face was all heart, thought Poppy.

'I shall not be staying in here long. He has to be moved to the Condemned Cell, as well you know. Now please, let us talk and pray alone.'

The chaplain spoke softly at first to the trembling man.

'You know Weeks that I have been praying for your soul, asking the Almighty for his tender mercy on a miserable sinner who has done great wrong.'

'Thank you sir, but I'm an innocent man, God help me.'

Matthew Weeks could barely stand.

'I did not kill her, sir. You must believe me. The courts have got it all wrong. Lies were told about me.'

His voice dropped away to a whisper.

Poppy had to strain to hear his words.

'They all say they're innocent in here, Weeks,' said Kendall, drily. 'But enough of this. I come to pray with you, man. To prepare you for your final journey, for when you come face to face with the Lord. There will be no untruths in the next world. Remember God's commandments *Thou shalt not bear false witness* and, even more relevant in this case, *Thou shalt not kill*. Are you a chapel-goer or church, Weeks?'

'Church back home in Lezant, sir. But Tremail Chapel when I'm at the farm with the mistress's family, sir.'

Matthew's whisper was barely audible now.

'Well it's time we prayed together, Weeks, before you write your formal confession.'

Kendall put on his most pious expression.

'But I can't make no confession sir!'

Matthew looked bewildered.

'I didn't murder Charlotte Dymond, sir. 'Twas someone else who done it, someone who lied in the court after taking a Bible oath!'

Matthew's voice was stronger now, pleading his case.

'An' I can't write my letters anyways, sir. Nor 'ardly read at all.'

'Quiet, Weeks. The Lord hears all your wickedness.

98

The court has proven you guilty and you will hang for it.'

A low moan escaped from Matthew and he dropped to his knees, like the ox before the manger.

Kendall continued, more gently now.

'It is the requirement of the law of this land that you make your confession to this most heinous crime. Your confession will be written and pinned on the gaol gate for all to see, after you have gone to meet your Maker.'

Another low moan came from Matthew Weeks.

'Now let us pray, to the Lord who is Merciful...'

Poppy stood there, staring at the wretched man who was weeping.

'I can't breathe, I must get out of here.'

Poppy pushed past, panic-stricken, out into the clean air. The cell and the tragic scene faded quickly.

And there stood a puzzled Annie in front of her, in the small patch of the cottage garden, her eyes deeply troubled.

TWENTY ONE

THE day's outing, which should have been enjoyable, passed off in a strained atmosphere. Annie drove and Poppy chain-smoked silently the whole way. Annie had desperately attempted to make 'ordinary' conversation but it was tough-going. They descended the hill into Truro and the three spires and the copper tower of the cathedral pierced the opaque clouds before them.

'If only we could pierce this God-awful atmosphere,' thought Annie as she attempted to manoeuvre her car into the small space between two shiny, silver BMWs, which had arrogantly parked over the lines.

Truro was busy as usual, its streets packed with people. Annie sorted out some cash for a parking ticket and wished once again that she was at home relaxing on her precious day off. Poppy got out and ground a half-smoked cigarette under the heel of her boot. She stuck her hands deep into her jacket of terracotta wool and looked mutinous.

'Right, let's hit the shops. Or would you rather have a coffee first?'

Annie was doing her best to be normal.

'Tea,' was the monosyllabic response.

'Well tea, then... and sugary doughnuts oozing jam.'

'Whatever,' was Poppy's exasperating reply.

They found a tea shop in a narrow alleyway. Talk between them was difficult. They drank their tea and ate doughnuts in silence. Poppy was making patterns in the spilled sugar on the table with her finger. Annie had tried, and failed, to make conversation. Poppy was withdrawn and morose. At last something in Annie snapped.

'Why are you being so bloody?'

Poppy looked up from her sugary swirls and faced her angry friend across the table.

'I didn't ask to come to Truro on a useless day out. I told you I didn't want to.'

Poppy's eyes glittered dangerously.

'But no. You wouldn't listen. You had to interfere as usual.'

Her voice was becoming more strident; it grew even louder. A couple at another table turned to look at them.

'Look! I am trying to help you for what it's worth.'

Annie gripped Poppy's thin wrist urgently across the table.

'I know you've been through a terrible time,' she said, 'but you are starting to lose your grip on everyday reality. Look at what happened back at your cottage earlier. You had a panic attack, just like you did the other night at the party. You need to get some help.'

Poppy stood up and glared coldly down at Annie, still sitting amidst the sugar, the globules of jam and slops of tea.

'Don't you dare tell me to get a grip on anything,' she hissed. 'Matt is dead. The man I loved is dead. I can't stop seeing his broken body on the rocks below me, moving with the tide.'

She wrenched herself away from the messy table, past the staring customers and out into the thoroughfare. By the time Annie had paid the bill and followed her into a side street, Poppy was halfway through smoking a badly-rolled cigarette.

'Now what?'

Annie's voice sounded as hurt as she looked.

'I actually need to do some shopping while we are

here. I suggest we go off on our own for a while and meet at the car in a couple of hours. It'll give us both time to calm down.'

Poppy blew smoke into the air and nodded.

'Fine,' she said.

She wandered off alone through the crowds of shoppers, rather aimlessly at first. Her sudden rage had subdued and feelings of guilt about her treatment of Annie were coming to the surface. She beat them back down.

Then she found a flea market in an echoing hall and browsed some piles of books. There was the familiar smell of ancient mustiness in the air. Some of the older books had plain leather covers, spotted with mould and mildew. They felt damp to the touch. She picked up a small book of Victorian poetry in a soft suede cover and read a few lines. She put it back down and meandered on between the stalls. Then she noticed a jumbled Cornish section. The clay-country writings of Jack Clemo rubbed dust-jackets with A L Rowse and the great 'Q' himself. Charles Causley's *Hands To Dance And Skylark* nestled next to Daphne du Maurier's *Loving Spirit,* all in a wonderful sense of disarray. A collection of short stories seemed to draw Poppy's attention. A whisper seemed to come from inside her head

'Pick it up. Turn the pages.'

She held the book, which had a green and blue illustrated dust-jacket, reading its title aloud.

'*Staircase to the Sea.*'

Cornish cliffs and a seascape seemed an apt enough design, she thought. It was sub-titled *Fourteen Ghost Stories From Cornwall.*

'Looks a good read.'

The book-seller smiled at her, rubbed his cold fingers together and blew on them.

'Do you want to take it?'

She shook her head and put it back on the stall.

'Take it,' whispered a small voice out of the darkness in her mind.

The man on the stall had already turned away and was unscrewing a flask of something hot to drink. Poppy picked the book up again and stroked the cover, with its dramatic scene of cliffs and turbulent sea. A moon drifted through the clouds, casting an eerie light on desolate mine shafts and engine houses and, in the distance, on a ruined barn with a skeletal roof and a silhouetted church tower.

'Take it. It will lead you to me,' whispered the voice.

She knew, of course, that she would see no one behind her if she turned. Yet the voice was familiar. A voice, one of several, which haunted her dreams on lonely nights at Penhale Cottage. In something of a trance Poppy turned a few pages until she found the Contents page. She skimmed the list of stories. A tiny smile crept to the corners of her mouth as she read one title, *Poppy Time*.

She was meant to read this book then. She reached somewhat shakily for her purse deep in the pocket of her jeans and counted out some coins and a tattered ten-pound note. The book lay before her on top of a pile of paperbacks.

'I've never heard of the writer James Turner before,' she said, as the book-seller put his cup on a chair with some alacrity to take the money from her.

'I think he had a local background. Lived somewhere near the north coast.'

He wrapped the book in a brown paper bag.

'He liked writing about spirits and stuff, all that sort of thing.'

'Thanks,' said Poppy, taking her purchase and

holding it in both hands, clutching it to her chest. She made her way out of the echoing market and turned, without thinking, towards the cathedral. She needed somewhere quiet where she would be able to sit and think. Whatever had made her think the cathedral would be quiet? As she climbed the steps to the western door a crowd of schoolgirls in uniform came clattering down the steps, ties askew and chattering like magpies.

But as she slipped through the doorway she soon became aware of the quiet hush of a sacred place. Candles flickered in a dark recess and high, high above her in the nave were the flutes of the fan-vaulting. Footsteps trod quietly past her as she made her way to a dim corner where she could sit, uninterrupted. The book in its paper bag lay on her lap as she sat quietly, absorbing the calm atmosphere all around her. She closed her eyes and could hear her own breathing gradually slowing and becoming regular. She felt at peace.

When her eyes opened she realised she must have slept a little, and the book had slipped from her lap on to the stone floor. She picked it up and pulled it gently from its wrapping, staring again at the dust-jacket with its moon-blanched Cornish picture. The book fell open at the words *Charlotte, you can't leave me forever...*

In that very moment she knew that she had once again been led back to the moors and the ghost of Charlotte Dymond.

TWENTY TWO

THE wind was blowing gently, causing ripples to flow in the long grass down towards the ford. Above was the granite face of Roughtor, frowning down from its stone-strewn heights. In the distance a moving blur could be seen, either dark cattle or evidence of humans walking across the lower slopes. A grey-haired farmer, leaning on an old wooden gate, watched the distant movement with apparent interest. His black cattle were feeding contentedly on the hay he had lugged in an ancient horse-drawn cart, now standing on higher ground above the ford on the Camelford side of the stream. He chewed on a piece of grass as he watched the moving shapes intently.

It was late afternoon, the sun was already low in the sky. Visibility on the moor did not have the clarity of the earlier hours, yet the farmer stuck to his post, just like one of the sentries who would stand watch there many years later in wartime. The moving blur was becoming clearer now, evolving into the shapes of a woman, dressed in a long old-fashioned gown of many colours, with a man limping by her side. A tinkling sound of laughter could be heard above the sighing of the wind as the couple made their way slowly down towards the stream, picking their way carefully through the mud.

''Tis that Matthew Weeks,' observed the farmer to himself at the gate. 'I'd knaw his walk anywhere, the way he lurches an' all.'

He spat out the chewed piece of grass and crouched behind a stone wall, peeping out secretly, never taking his eyes off the couple. More laughter could be heard from the young woman, for now he could see quite clearly that she was indeed hardly more than a girl, with tendrils of black hair escaping from her rusty silk bonnet.

'And 'tis the milk-maid, Charlotte, from Penhale Farm with him,' he muttered to himself. 'Pretty maid too, though a bit spirited for my liking. I remember when her wouldn't stop laughing at Tremail Chapel one Sunday. Made a proper spectacle of herself that day. Mistress Peter was some angry with the maid that day. I reckon 'er got a right thrashing back at Penhale afterwards.'

'Charlotte!'

A plaintive voice called over the stream.

'Wait for me, Charlotte.'

More teasing laughter, carried from the stream-side.

'The maid's just playing with 'en,' sneered Isaac Cory, for such was the man's name. ''Tis right that the minister denounced her as a whore for laughing in chapel. And she looked it, with her red lips and wearing that red shawl. She wasn't brought up proper. But then her mother wasn't much better, by all accounts.'

He peered round the end of the wall. Now the couple were face-to-face, talking earnestly. Snippets of their conversation were carried on the air. The tones of the man's deeper voice sounded distressed and Cory smiled in enjoyment.

'Serves 'im right. Never did see eye-to-eye with Matthee Weeks, ever since I was taken on for a time as herdsman by Mistress Peter.'

He paused and preened to himself.

'Still, I'm me own man now. Small farmer. Got me own acres of land up at Trevilian's Gate.'

Once again he sneaked a look around the gate-post. He frowned and muttered.

''Tis getting a bit foggy up top of Roughtor. I should

be having a quick look at me wheat field afore I go home.'

He seemed torn between going home and staying put to continue spying on the youngsters.

'No Matthew!'

The girl's voice rang out clearly.

Cory's greying head shot up over the stones of the wall, his eyes narrowing.

'Give me back my letter!'

Charlotte's pretty face was pinker now, with apparent anger.

'You know you can't even read it for yourself.'

She snatched at the letter, which Matthew held aloft in his upraised hand.

''Tis only from Rebecca, on the farm out to Blisland.'

She held out her hand.

'You've no need to be jealous Matthee,' she said more gently, stroking his blue cloth jacket.

Matthew reluctantly gave the letter to the girl after her persuasive appeal.

'Well 'tis strange that your letter arrived this morning, on the Sabbath, straight after Thomas Prout paid a visit to Penhale.'

His voice dropped away to nothing. His next words were lost. Isaac Cory strained to listen more closely. He had just heard his nephew's name, Tommy Prout, mentioned.

That did it. He would watch the couple for a bit longer, for who could tell what would happen next? Charlotte was holding on to Matthew's arm now, but his face was turned away from her. They were talking in lower, softer tones.

'Damnation!'

Cory's face was flushed and agitated.

'Speak up you pair,' he muttered to himself. 'What are you saying about my nephew, Tommy?'

His wheat field was all but forgotten. All was quiet for some long minutes, the only sounds being the trickling of the water and the far-off bleating of sheep and lambs on the slopes of the tor.

'Seems too quiet for my liking,' grunted Cory.

He peered around the granite gateway. Matthew Weeks stood alone, like a pillar of stone, by the stream. He was watching the figure of Charlotte, in her best bonnet and scarlet shawl, making her way to higher ground. She was holding her skirts above the soft marsh and testing out the clods of drier ground in her pattens.

'Charlotte! Don't go!'

His shouts were carried on the wind, but whether the girl heard them or not, she carried on her uphill climb.

'Don't leave me, Charlotte!' Matthew shouted desperately, hands cupped around his mouth. 'That Tommy Prout will never love you like I do.'

But Charlotte's small figure was becoming lost to him in the fog, which was falling in a white veil from the heights of Roughtor. How long Matthew stood there, a grief-stricken figure staring into the mist, is hard to say. Isaac Cory watched him, smiling grimly as he enjoyed Matthew's obvious distress.

'Serves Weeks right for arguing with me over them lost bullocks at Penhale. I'll never forgive 'en for telling tales on me to Mistress Peter.'

He licked his lips and plucked a fresh piece of grass.

'Seems like the whore has taken a fancy to our Tommy in his place.'

Smiling to himself, he made his way to his horse, its harness creaking with the sturdy mare's movements.

'Time to look at me wheat and get home to the missus.'

TWENTY THREE

POPPY was back at Penhale. Annie had dropped her off after their blighted trip to Truro. They had sat in her car briefly, talking again and both making a real attempt to put their earlier words and anger behind them. It was crazy for two close friends to fall out in such difficult days, they agreed.

Poppy stood in front of the cottage and waved as Annie drove away down the twisting lane. She watched until the car was out of sight and turned towards the porch. A glimpse of the great sun low on the line of the moors took her breath. It was so beautiful out here. Daylight was fading, birds were flying to the wooded areas to roost. Far away in the approaching twilight, a bullock was helving mournfully. She breathed deeply, glad to be back in the tranquil setting of the moorland, away from the bright lights and ringing of tills. Worse still, the constant, deafening roar of traffic.

That evening, sitting by a crackling fire with Winston purring on her knee, Poppy started to flick through James Turner's collection of stories. This time she was drawn immediately to one entitled *Love Affair* which had mesmerised her in the flea market earlier that day.

As she read the first page or two, Poppy quickly realised that the writer was consumed by his love for Charlotte Dymond. In effect Turner was in love with her ghost. How absurd, she thought. She picked up her brandy goblet and swirled the oily liquid around before taking another mouthful. But was it so absurd, she asked herself. Here, in the writing, was the agony and the longing for a much-loved, delightful girl of eighteen. Yet this was something different, for the beloved was dead, and had been since the year 1844.

What was so strange about being in love with a ghost? After all, she was in love with Matt's ghost if you believed the words of Josh. The difference was that Matt seemed lost to her. Just occasionally she would think she caught a glimpse of him in the shadows, his eyes full of sorrow. She would call his name and reach out to him, but he would soon be gone back into the shadows. If only she could touch him.

Poppy read the second page again, shaking her head. She understood the passion and the longing in the writing, but something was not right. She took another gulp of brandy and read the page again. There was the usual mention of Charlotte's death taking place on Sunday 14th April; then the undisputed fact that she was buried in the churchyard at Davidstow. But the writer was adamant. He knew for sure her jealous lover had, in fact, murdered Charlotte. Matthew Weeks had slit her throat near the ford at the bottom of Roughtor. He knew, he said, because her ghost had taken him there. James Turner had witnessed her fate, her violent death and release. Her blood had even splashed on to his jacket.

Yet to Poppy this version of events did not ring true. A voice in her head was telling her it was based on lies. Matthew Weeks was innocent. She had spent time with Matthew, seen just how much he had loved Charlotte in spite of her mocking laughter and wicked ways. She had seen him in his workplace on the farm, walking out on the moor, in the Assize Court. And she had seen the shadow of his former self, suffering in his cell at the gaol, with the prospect of the hangman's noose hanging over him. But if Matthew Weeks had not killed Charlotte

Dymond, then who had? He was a scapegoat, said a small voice in her head. Someone had to pay. A simple country girl, with a pretty face and name, had died violently. The farming community had been appalled. Chapel folk were riddled with guilt that they had not treated her better. She had been denounced as a whore. Her own mother had even threatened to kill her, was the rumour on the moor. Whatever people thought at the time, they had erected a stone monument in Charlotte's memory on the very spot her body had been found. A granite pillar, set in the marshy ground near the ford. Yet quite a grand memorial for a farm girl, who had laughed irreverently and been branded a whore by the minister at Tremail chapel. Something was not right. Had there been some sort of cover-up in 1844?

Poppy poured another brandy and cupped it in her hands. She stared into the flickering fire, her book put on one side now. Outside the wind was beginning to get up, its melancholy moaning creating a dreary atmosphere. But it was cosy by the fire, with the lamps giving off a soft glow. Winston padded over from a corner and found a comfortable place on the woollen hearth-rug. He began washing himself with his rough tongue, before settling down for a nap, purring loudly.

'Next time I'll come back as a cat,' thought Poppy, watching his contentment.

She reached over to the wicker basket and threw another log on the fire. Flames curled around it, hungrily licking its bone-dry bark. She stared into the brilliant orange and red flames, seeing pictures in the dark caves between the charred sticks and half-burned logs…

A girl with a laughing mouth, pulling her red shawl tightly around her shoulders. A man limping through the marshes, disappearing into the white mist. A woman's body lying in the marshy ground, her neck savagely cut.

A murder of crows flapping over the body in that lonely desolate spot, cawing harshly. An older man watching, watching from a gateway, with malice in his eyes. All these and more came to her, snapshots from another time and place.

How long she had been sitting there she could not tell, but the fire had gradually burned down leaving a red glow amongst the ashes. Outside the wind continued its moaning and wailing around the corners of the squat cottage.

Poppy suddenly sat bolt upright. The man with the greying hair, crouching in the gateway. She had not seen him before. Who was this new face in the jigsaw of faces from 1844? He had been spying on something or someone down by the ford. She must warn Matthew and Charlotte...

How bloody crazy is that, she thought. How the hell could she warn them that they were being watched? They had both been dead for a century and a half.

She stood up to shake herself. The wind howled more loudly and a log shifted in the fireplace, creating a shower of tiny sparks. Winston looked up at her through sleepy slitted eyes from his warm place on the mat.

Poppy could hear Annie's voice earlier that day clearly saying: 'You are starting to lose your grip on reality... you need to get some help.'

She reached for her friend, the brandy bottle, now nearly empty, and poured the last drops into her glass with a shaky hand. No problem, there was another bottle hidden in the bedroom. As she turned to put the empty bottle down, Poppy caught a glimpse of her pale, thin face and dishevelled hair in the mirror. She was caught, framed in the mirror's wooden edges, looking like some terrible creature fished out of a Gothic novel. The mad woman locked in the attic. Bertha Rochester, with her wild hair, haunting the dark passages still looking for her lost love. Is this what she would become? A woman who has lost touch with the real world? Like Miss Havisham, decaying in her candle-lit house, in her stinking, yellowing wedding dress.

It was time to face up to things before it was too late. Annie was right. She needed some kind of help. She put the empty glass down purposefully and reached for her mobile phone. She started to scroll down through the list of names.

Then she heard a whispering from the darkness under the staircase.

'Let me help you, Poppy. You know I still love you. Don't be afraid. I will not hurt you.'

TWENTY FOUR

JOSH had not seen Poppy for several days. He had been inundated with time-consuming jobs on the farm and his father had been increasingly angry at his sudden disappearances to Penhale just when he was most needed. His mother had spoken to him quietly in the farmhouse kitchen, voicing her worry that Josh would only get hurt if he kept seeing Poppy. It was obvious the girl 'had problems,' as she delicately put it. She had tucked a strand of stray silvering hair behind her ear, expecting some sort of irate reply from her eldest son. It soon came. She continued placidly peeling potatoes for the evening roast while Josh let rip to his pent-up feelings.

'That's not fair, mum. You know what a bloody awful time she's had these past months.'

His weathered face looked ashen under his freckles.

'She's out there in that old cottage on the edge of the moor, all on her own. She needs someone to give her a bit of support.'

'Well that was her decision Josh, to live in such an isolated place.'

She paused from her peeling, the dripping knife in her hand.

'Your dad said she was crazy when she moved out there. Now she seems to be taking up all your time, sapping your energy. When did you last have a good night out with your friends?'

Josh had a face like thunder.

'Poppy is not crazy! You've never liked her, that's

the truth of it. Not even when we were at school. Or dad, come to that. If it was up to dad I'd be settled down by now with some girl from the Young Farmers Club with big breasts and acres of land.'

His mother had to smile to herself at that. Josh yanked his jacket noisily off the peg by the door and an ancient sheep-dog raised his head from the mat in front of the Rayburn.

'I'm off out. Tell dad I'll be back later.'

The door slammed behind him. The old dog settled once more. His mother sighed and went back to her potatoes by the sink. Josh drove off furiously, splashing puddles of filthy water over his father who was emerging from the newly renovated barn, a grim expression on his face.

The jeep made its way up the high-sided muddy lane and turned on to the main road towards Launceston. The light was already fading and the rain had become Cornish drizzle, misting visibility across the landscape. Eerily the white blades of the huge windmills appeared out of the greyness. Swearing loudly, he pulled in to the verge. Where was he going? He seemed to lack all sense of direction these days. Perhaps his mother was right, he should meet up with some friends. It was a bit early for that, but no doubt there would be a friendly face and a cheering fire in his local. Yes, a pint was just what he needed right now.

The pint became several pints. Outside it was pitch-black when he eventually wobbled out to the car park. The wind had got up and the drizzle had stopped while he was in the warm of the bar. Where should he go now? Home to another row with his bad-tempered father, followed by looks of mild disapproval from his mum? No, he would drive out to see Poppy, and to hell with the lot of them.

Josh approached the cottage with his stomach churning. The yellow square of light seemed to shine more brightly than usual, the twisted trees were thrashing about in the strong winds. He pulled up by the gate, which was unfastened and banging to and fro in the wind.

He climbed unsteadily out of the jeep and shut the gate on its latch behind him as he paused in the wild piece of garden. Poppy would be pleased to see him, he reassured himself. After all, she must get fed up with being a recluse. He stood under the stone porch, bracing himself to knock the door. Despite the shriek of the wind, he thought he could hear voices coming from inside the cottage. He found it hard to believe she had company on a night like this. Only Poppy's old car was parked nearby, somewhat haphazardly, on the grass verge. Or was it sheer possessiveness on his part, thought Josh, not wanting to believe that she had a life that did not include him?

He put his ear flat against the door. Yes, there were definitely two voices he could hear and one was that of a man. He stood back, as if he had been scalded. Should he go away? It was then he heard the terrible sobbing as the wind lulled.

'Please don't, don't leave me again. I can't bear it.'

The wind moaned loudly. The yellow light from the window was fading gradually.

'You say you will help me. Help me then, I beg you. You won't even let me touch you.'

Again that terrible crying or keening, like a death lament. Josh felt freezing cold. He was sober in an instant. He knocked on the door so loudly it hurt his knuckles and made them bleed.

'Poppy? It's Josh. Are you OK?'

Silence from within. The only sound the wailing

wind as it blasted around the strong walls. Again a loud knocking from Josh. Silence.

Minutes later, which seemed like hours to him, the door opened, just a crack. A hoarse whisper from Poppy,

'What do you want?'

He got a glimpse of her white face and a mass of dishevelled wild hair. There were violet shadows under her red, tearful eyes.

'Can I come in? It's blowing a gale out here.'

His own voice sounded different somehow.

'I've come to see how you are.'

There was a pause and then the cottage door opened slowly. Poppy stood behind it as he entered. There was a strong smell of unusual perfume in the shadowy room. And what had happened to the bright yellow light he had seen as he was driving down the track? The room was cold. And it was empty. He turned to look at her. He was shocked. It was only a few days since he had seen her, but she looked gaunt. If she had been thin before, now she looked almost skeletal in the shadows. Her green eyes had lost all their sparkle. She looked ill, drained of all life, with her tangled hair and transparent skin.

'What's happened to your fire?' he asked, to cover the awkward moment. 'I'll soon get it going again.'

He knelt by the hearth and sorted some kindling, glad to be doing something practical. Poppy wavered behind him, like a wraith, in the darkness.

'Were you talking to someone? I could swear I heard voices when I was outside,' he asked in a casual tone, with his back to her. A flame flickered and grew.

'No. Not really.'

Her response was quiet, vague.

'But I thought I heard a man's voice Poppy,' he persisted. 'Is there someone here?'

Visions of a secret lover hiding upstairs came to him

in a red mist, as he puffed and blew on the fire. He looked back at her over his shoulder. She stood, glimmering in the flickering light, twisting her scarf in her thin white hands.

'Matt was here,' she said, and sighed. 'But he's gone now.'

A cold feeling crept over Josh, even the flames he had been coaxing into life could not warm him in that moment.

'I know what you are going to say. Matt is dead.'

Her voice was a mere whisper.

'But he was here with me.'

She wept openly now.

'I begged him to stay with me, and now he's gone and I can't bear it.'

She looked so thin and tragic that Josh stood up and folded her into his comforting embrace. She laid her head on his chest, inhaling the sweet smell of hay on his old jumper.

'Sssh... it's all right, darling.'

Never a romantic, Josh used the term of endearment to his own amazement.

'I'm here now to look after you.'

She closed her eyes and, as always, felt secure in his arms.

TWENTY FIVE

THE postman's van came meandering down the lane towards Penhale Cottage. Josh watched it draw up outside. He drew back behind the curtains, not wanting that gossipy Batten bloke to see him on his rounds. Bugger! His jeep was parked outside. No doubt the whole postal round would be informed that Josh Clemo had slept the night with that weird red-haired girl at Penhale Cottage. Poppy was still upstairs in bed, sleeping the sleep of the exhausted. He had not gone home to St Clether the night before. He knew his father would be savage about more missed work, so he'd sent his mum a cowardly text explaining that there had been an emergency. He'd be back later, he'd said, to sort things out.

Some junk mail plopped on the mat. Josh picked it up and saw that there was also a letter from America with it. He frowned. That was probably from Poppy's mum, he thought. Fat lot of good she was as a mother. She'd swanned off to the States without a backward glance, and in no time at all she'd married some rich bloke in Texas. He thought of the contrast to his own mother: working on the farm in busy seasons, forever baking cakes and making pasties, helping family and friends whenever she could.

He made a mug of strong black coffee and decided not to take one up to Poppy. Hopefully sleep would help her. She had looked ill, really ill, last night. And when he had held her, she was nothing but skin and bone. The problem was, what should he do next? He sipped his coffee. He had a bloody awful headache from his session at the pub. Food might help him think.

The cat needed to be fed too. Winston was nuzzling his legs and making a pathetic yowling to attract attention. He sighed and looked in the cupboard. He pushed several tins of slimmers' soup to one side and found some cat nibbles at the back. Winston looked at them in his dish with contempt, then resignedly proceeded to crunch his way through. Like a pig eating ashes, his granny would have said. Josh found some old-looking crackers and some ripe stilton which was crying to be thrown out, but he needed to eat something. Anything. Poppy was obviously neglecting her food intake as well as everything else, he thought, for her cupboards were bare. He stood by the window eating the soggy crackers, looking out across the moor. What was out there, he wondered, that was having such an unnerving effect on Poppy?

The sun was shining weakly after the storm of the night before. The whole scene was peaceful, of nature at its best. Why then did she keep imagining things, people even. This thing about Matt for instance, what a load of old cobblers that was.

Yet in that instant he remembered something he had forgotten in his semi-drunk state the night before... the voices inside the cottage. Two voices. And one had been clearly that of a man. But when he entered the cottage it had been empty, apart from Poppy herself. There had been an unusual smell of perfume, a strong musky odour he called to mind. The yellow light had dimmed and the fire had virtually died out, and there was a tangible coldness in the air.

As he mused by the window, Poppy appeared silently behind him. She put a cold white hand on his shoulder. He started at the touch. She stood next to him by the window, searching the lonely landscape. She sighed deeply and leaned her head on his broad shoulder. He looked down at her,

'What is it, Poppy? What is happening to you? You can tell me anything, you know that by now.'

She sighed once more and turned from him.

'You wouldn't believe me anyway.'

'Try me.'

'I tried to tell you last night that Matt came here.'

She faced him. Josh gave a small, forced smile.

'We talked. He told me not to be afraid. He said he still loved me.'

Poppy twisted the silver ring on her finger.

'But he told me that I could not touch him.'

She stood shivering in her cotton nightdress.

'And then you knocked at the door and he was gone. Gone in an instant.'

Josh tried to picture what had happened. He pulled her towards him. For the second time in twenty-four hours he held her shivering body firmly in his solid embrace.

'Look Poppy,' he said firmly. 'You need to get dressed in some warm clothes. Then we both need to get something decent to eat.'

Poppy tried to disentangle herself, but Josh held her tightly.

'Then we'll talk about it some more, later on.'

She looked up at him.

'Promise?'

'Promise,' Josh said, trying to sound nonchalant about the whole thing.

His jeep splashed through the lane and ground across the cattle grid, away from the moor. The silence between them was a fairly comfortable one, he thought, congratulating himself on getting Poppy away from

Penhale for a few hours. He knew he ought to get home to the farm, but that would just have to wait. Inside an hour the jeep was pulling up near the quay in Padstow. Gulls wheeled and cried, heckling over some fishy scraps dumped near a bin.

A few early holidaymakers meandered by the harbour in the spring sunshine. There was a smell of boats and tar and yacht varnish in the air. A few smaller boats were moored by the harbour wall, bobbing on the lilting water. For a while they could be like a normal couple, Josh thought, as they walked along the quay together. They stopped and watched some boys fishing for crabs by the slippery steps. It was invigorating to feel a sense of freedom in the fresh sea air, away from the darkly intense, clinging atmosphere of Poppy's cottage. He watched her closely, hoping it was doing her some good. They sat on a bench eating fish and chips, watching the scene of boats being overhauled and people going about their daily tasks. There was a smell of fresh paint as cottages and flats overlooking the harbour were given a final face-lift before the holiday season started in earnest.

'Do you know what really makes me mad about Padstow?'

Poppy spoke her thoughts out loud as she looked across the harbour.

'It's all those folk who call it Pad-stein. I know Rick Stein has created jobs here with his fish restaurants and stuff, but Padstow was here and on the map a long time before he ever came here. Lets face it, he's just an emmet to the locals.'

Josh grinned and mumbled in agreement. He wiped his mouth with the back of his hand.

'Too right! A mate of mine is a true Padstonian, born and bred. Peace Oss supporter. He reckons most of the real locals would kick him into touch if they could.'

They sat, musing in the warmth of the sunshine, watching the world go by. There was the silence of friends, a comfortable, relaxed feeling, which Josh felt recently he might have lost forever. Poppy stood up and brushed a tiny glistening piece of batter off her jacket.

'Let's walk a bit further.'

Josh nodded.

Together they strolled to the further harbour wall and watched a boat battling its way over from Rock on the other side of the estuary. Out there was the notorious Doom Bar. A chillier wind was blowing, summer was still some way off. Yet it was only a matter of a couple of weeks and Padstow would be decked out in her flags and greenery, its streets crammed with people in blue and red spotted scarves and sashes singing the May Song to a hypnotic beat of the drums. The weird gyrations of its two Obby Osses through its narrow streets would celebrate May Day with the singing of the age-old words

'Summer has a-come unto day.'

They meandered up the path towards the war memorial and hunched themselves into their coat collars as the wind blew with more strength. Below them was the wild, green sea with white horses dancing on its peaks. The tide looked as if it was about to turn. Poppy's eyes were glittering with a bright intensity as she turned to look at Josh.

'I've just remembered some beautiful words from the Celtic Blessing,' she said loudly, above the buffeting of the wind.

'Deep peace of the running wave to you.
Deep peace of the flowing air to you.'

Josh raised his voice too.

'And what about you? Do you feel at peace?'

'Yes,' she said simply. 'Here and now I do, more than I have for weeks.'

She tucked her arm under his and gazed out to sea. Her words were carried on the wind.

'I am away from the brooding moors, working their weird magic on me.'

He looked down at her by his side. The wind was whipping her wild red hair around her face like that of some fierce maenad. She looked up quickly and gave him a rare, brilliant smile. They started back down the path towards the shelter of Padstow and its bustling harbour.

TWENTY SIX

ON her return from Padstow, refreshed and with some colour in her blanched cheeks, Poppy ripped open the letter from America. She skimmed it quickly, sighed loudly, and threw it on the table. A strong waft of perfumed hyacinths came from the window. She was drawn towards the light, fading fast over the line of the moors. Birds were flying low in flocks, silhouetted against the rosy sky.

'It's going to be a much colder night,' she said to a purring Winston by her side.

The letter she had thrown down so dismissively was, of course, from her mother, Angie. It was bursting with snippets of her fantastically changed life in the States, with new husband, Brad. The letter reeked of expensive perfume and the high life; it was a list of celebrities she was rubbing shoulder-pads with at dinner parties, designer clothes, jewellery and exhausting days of pampering. A glossy photo of her mother was enclosed, with immaculate sun-streaked hair and expensive sunglasses, holding a cocktail glass as she lazed by a swimming pool. Only at the end of the letter had there been the remotest sign of interest as to how her only daughter might be coping.

'You know how we would love it, sweetheart, if you came out to stay with us. Brad would be just made up! He would spoil you rotten, just like he does me.'

Then a postscript: 'I am not Angie any more. That name was part of my old life. He calls me Angel. Isn't that sweet?'

'Actually it makes me want to vomit,' Poppy muttered savagely to herself, as she knelt to sort out the dead fire, raking out the ashes with sudden venom. Once the fire was lit, she carried the ashes outside to add to the growing ash-pile behind the cottage. The early evening light was fading. She felt strangely peaceful, happy even for the first time in ages as she stood for a minute or so absorbing the beauty of the clear outline of the moors. Then as she turned to go back into the cottage, she was jolted by what she saw. A lonely figure stood, watching, in the distance. The figure of a woman.

'Charlotte,' she whispered to herself, under her breath.

Then much louder she called: 'Charlotte! Can you hear me?'

The figure remained quite, quite still. Despite the chilly evening air, she was dressed in an old-fashioned gown and her neck was bare, apart from a necklace of beads, which took on the red light.

'What do you want?'

Poppy moved away from the doorway.

'Come closer.'

The young woman did not move.

'Let me help you, Charlotte. Why can't your spirit be at rest?'

She shook her head slowly, tendrils of her hair moving as if in a breeze around her beautiful face. She turned away, looking back over her shoulder as she moved further into the purple shadows created by the weird-shaped stones of the moor.

Poppy watched, trembling, as the figure faded into the heart of the moor's darkness. She must have stood there for several minutes, unconsciously clutching the tin ash bucket. The haunting sound of a bird calling eerily somewhere across the marshes in the dusk brought her out of her reverie.

'She's gone.'

Poppy shivered, suddenly aware of the cold air. She pushed open the cottage door and was rewarded with cheering lamplight and the fire flickering in the hearth. The door tightly bolted behind her, Poppy squatted on the rug and held her hands out to the growing warmth.

'I'm not afraid, this time.'

She stroked Winston's soft black fur, as he sat contentedly before the firelight.

'But why is she haunting me? It is as if she is trying to tell me something, across all the years.'

She thought long and hard, well into the evening. She read Causley's beautiful ballad yet again. The last three verses asked the reader the question: which of the two lovers, Charlotte or Matthew, deserves your prayers the most?

'They are both dead and gone. They have been dead since 1844, so why can't they simply stay dead?'

She rolled a cigarette and reached for a book, flicking through some marked pages.

'Charlotte was found dead by the ford at Roughtor. She was found in shallow water, marshy ground. Locals said the ground around her had been churned up by cattle, in a ring round the turf where she bled to death. How weird is that?'

Poppy scanned the page in front of her.

'And another strange thing, the crows flew up in a flock as the search party approached her, but her body was untouched. Everyone knows what crows are like; given the chance they'll peck out the eyes of a sheep in no time.'

She lit the cigarette.

'Then a few months later poor Matthew died in Bodmin Gaol, by hanging.'

She stopped again, got up, and walked up and down the small room, restlessly.

'What I want to really know is, why does she keep coming back to walk the moors, to haunt me? Why won't she rest?'

She went to the window and looked out into the darkness.

'Is it that only Charlotte knows what really happened that day?'

She could see the glow of her cigarette reflected in the window as she dragged on it.

'Or, is it that Matthew Weeks was nowhere near Roughtor ford late on that fateful April afternoon? In that case, who was there with Charlotte in his place? Tommy Prout? Or the man with malice in his eyes?'

She pulled the curtains across, shutting out the moor and all its dark secrets. Her phone rang as she was pouring herself a glass of red wine.

'Damn! Who the hell can that be? It won't be Josh, he said he had rugby training at Polson this evening.'

She rummaged in her bag for her mobile, but it was too late, it had stopped. She checked the missed call. Annie. A wave of guilt swept over her. She had given Annie a hard time at Truro. Perhaps she had better ring her back. Poppy gulped a mouthful of wine and tried to call her.

'Hey!'

Annie's voice was cheerful.

'I'm in Camelford at the moment. Been at some tedious arty-farty meeting. Fancy a bit of company for an hour?'

Poppy forced a bright tone.

'That would be great, Annie! See you soon then.'

She put another log on the fire and poured another glass of wine. She looked at Winston, leg extended, washing himself with his rough pink tongue in front of the fire.

'We've got company coming boy, so make the most of your spot by the fire while you can.'

Soon she heard a car outside. Poppy opened the door and the cold air infiltrated the cottage.

'It's brass monkeys out there.'

Annie's face was reddened with the cold and she wore layers of bright woollen clothes. Her nose had a drip that shone in the light. Poppy watched it with fascination, wondering how long it would be before it fell. Annie made a bee-line for the sofa by the fire. Winston slunk quickly into the shadows with a malevolent backward glance. Poppy handed her a glass and sat on the fireside chair next to the log-basket.

'It's really lovely in here, Poppy. Really cosy with the brass lamps and the wonderful fire.'

Annie grinned at her as she sipped her wine.

'Mmm, nice plonk. But I mustn't have too much, I'm driving.'

Poppy smiled secretly to herself as she thought back to a few days before, when Annie had described her home as 'an awful bloody place... may as well be in a prison cell'.

'Yes I like my quaint little shepherd's cottage, even if it is a bit too isolated at times. But Winston keeps me company. Don't you, boy?'

'You look a bit more like your old self tonight, Poppy. What have you been up to? Anything nice? There's even some colour in your cheeks.'

'Not as much as in your cheeks, Annie. Have you looked in a mirror lately?'

Poppy took a gulp of Shiraz before putting her glass down and getting out her tobacco.

'Anyway, Josh took me to Padstow today. It took me by surprise, but I enjoyed it. We had fish 'n' chips by the harbour and walked a bit and did some wave-watching.'

'Brilliant! Good old Josh to get you out and about.'

Annie sipped her wine, observing Poppy closely over the rim of her glass.

'He's a star.'

The friends talked for a while, Annie about her stressful job in Child Protection for Social Services; Poppy about her new determination to get to grips with her life now that Matt had gone.

'I must pick up his ashes and put them somewhere special,' she said softly. 'I keep putting it off, but I know I have to do it.'

'You will feel better when you've actually done it.'

Annie's voice was gentle.

'Where do you think you will put them?'

'Maybe somewhere near St Ives; we met there by the lifeboat station.'

'Why not have them taken out to sea on the lifeboat and scattered? I knew someone who had that done. He always said he didn't want a gravestone for people to gawp at. He wanted to be at one with the elements. To just disappear.'

'Perhaps.'

Poppy was wistful now. There was a lull in their conversation. Annie sipped her wine. Poppy rolled a cigarette slowly and thoughtfully.

'Do you think it is possible to be in love with a ghost?'

Annie put her glass down decisively.

'No I bloody well do not! What a load of old rubbish. Don't start thinking like that for goodness sake.'

'Actually I was not talking about myself.'

Poppy's voice was even quieter now.

'There was a local writer who used to live somewhere around here in North Cornwall. He believed he was in love with the ghost of Charlotte Dymond.'

Annie frowned, saying: 'As I said before, what a load of old rubbish.'

'Ah, but you see he was so obsessed with her that after his own death his ashes were scattered by Charlotte's monument on the moor.'

Poppy blew cigarette smoke towards the fireplace and watched it drift up the chimney.

'Will you help me find out what happened to Charlotte? I really need to know, Annie.'

She reached out and grasped her friend's hand.

'You see, Annie, she is haunting me too.'

TWENTY SEVEN

ANNIE left the dregs of wine in her glass, wrapping her scarves and woollen layers tightly around her against the cold night air. She had not said very much in reply to Poppy's plea for help, frowning so heavily that her eyebrows nearly met in the middle, like Dickens' Miss Murdstone.

'You know I think you're barking mad,' she had said in a muffled voice from the depths of a scarf. 'This girl you say you keep seeing is just a figment of your over-ripe imagination. And all this stuff about this bloke Matthew Weeks, who you are convinced was not her actual murderer... well, it's going to be hard to find out the truth now.'

Poppy followed her to the door.

'But I know that part is true. I know, in my heart, that Matthew did not kill Charlotte Dymond, and I am not the only one to think that. I feel sure she is trying to tell me something, to lead me somewhere. Why else would she keep coming here to Penhale?'

'God knows. No promises that we can ever find that out,' Annie said, her warm breath smoking on the cold air. She made her way to her car, which was sparkling with the late frost. 'But I am prepared to listen to your insane ramblings, even if no one else will.'

That night it was bitterly cold. Poppy banked up the fire and made up a warm bed downstairs on the sofa. She threw an extra couple of fleeces on the top, and Winston soon padded over and curled up by her side, purring loudly. She lay, drowsily watching the red glowing caves of the fire. Soon she felt relaxed and comfortable, a different person to the night before when Josh had found her, wailing and shivering, like someone demented. Her eyes closed and she slept.

She was out near Crowdy reservoir. It was freezing. The air was so cold it hurt when she breathed in. Everything sparkled with frost, like sugar. The reservoir was frozen, its surface gleaming in the strange light. She could see Brown Willy and Roughtor. In the middle of the frozen surface of the reservoir was a table, draped with snowy-white linen, topped with a red cloth. A bottle of wine and two filled glasses could clearly be seen on the tablecloth. A pair of metal chairs were arranged at the table, waiting for those who would risk dining in this winter wonderland. It was surreal.

She could hear the frosty grass crunching under her feet. She could smell the sharp pine-needles of the nearby plantation. An unseen voice called to her, echoing across the ice. Was it Matt's voice? Where was he? She could not see a soul on the lonely landscape.

'Meet me out on the ice. Come across to the other side. We can dine together,' said Matt's familiar voice ringing across the metallic-sounding ice.

Gingerly she put a foot on the edge. She could hear the hollow groan of the surface beneath her as she put her second foot on the ice. She knew it was senseless, but wouldn't she put her life at risk for her beloved Matt? She would skate into the middle and sit at the table with him. What did it matter that there was a warning sign, urging people not to venture on to the ice? What did it matter if the reservoir was fifty metres deep? She began to slide and skate towards the middle, unaware of the cracking sounds beneath her feet. She could look down and see bubbles and trailing weeds trapped in the frozen water. She knew she must reach the table, and drink the red wine he had poured for her. But she was so very cold, her feet were frozen. The table was almost within her reach when she saw it... a broken necklace scattered on the ice, its shining red beads like drops of blood. She woke in a cold sweat, totally disorientated.

'Charlotte's beads were on the ice,' she murmured. 'What the hell were they doing there?'

Poppy sat up. She rubbed her feet to warm them. The fire was a mere glow. She threw on a couple of dry sticks and watched them catch alight.

'I remember the ice was cracking, but Matt wanted me to cross over... to be with him.'

She bit her lip hard and tasted blood.

'He would not want to hurt me, I know that, but...'

She became aware of the warm softness of Winston's fur next to her cold feet, rubbing himself against her. Matt's cat, licking her freezing skin with his tongue. She stroked him and listened to his loud, ecstatic purring. She still had a piece of Matt to give her pleasure and to comfort her.

Warm once more in her nest by the fire, she drifted into a deep and dreamless sleep.

Outside, the moon was sailing above the tors' misshapen stones. Stars shone clearly in the night sky.

The moor's beauty was breath-taking on such a frosty night. Water froze in crevices in the rocks on the higher ground and even the marshy ground, rutted with the tracks of cattle, hardened with ice. A dog-fox slunk into the shadow of the gateway. A barn owl swooped for its prey, ghostly-white on silent wings. A tiny wisp of smoke from the cottage curled into the black sky, like a white feather.

Standing in the moon-blanched landscape near the old stone wall, was a lone figure. She stood without moving, while time passed by. Her features were shrouded in shadow, her head and shoulders hunched in a shawl against the bitter cold.

The figure watched the sleeping granite cottage. Its thin white plume of smoke an unfurled flag of surrender in the darkness.

Twenty Eight

CHARLOTTE Dymond had left the farm at Penhale on that afternoon, dressed in her Sunday-best clothes. She had walked out with Matthew Weeks. Nine days later, her body was found. Her throat had been cut. A broken necklace was found just behind Charlotte's head. There were pale stains on her gown, presumably her blood had been washed away by the river water. Her body was carried back across the moor on a cart to Penhale Farm.

Back home, one might say.

When they carried me back, I could hear them talking.

'There was no sign of a struggle,' *I heard one say.* 'But where's her shoes and her pattens?'

'I picked some of 'er beads up from the slope,' *said a younger man's voice.* 'Must 'ave been broke when 'e cut her throat.'

'Hand them to me. I'll take charge of they,' *said Mary Westlake. I recognised her voice, for she was the bossy daughter of Mrs Peter, my mistress at Penhale. The cart bumped noisily along the track. I was glad that I could not really feel it. I kept thinking of my green-striped gown all torn and askew, for all the world to see my stockings.*

'Come to that, they say the maid was wearing a bonnet and a shawl. Where be they, I wonder?'

I recognised the gravelly voice of William Northam, who kept the inn at Halworthy.

'And there were no weapon to be found by the body. P'raps he threw it into them marshes, near Crowdy.'

'Who be 'e talking about?' *asked Mary Westlake. I could imagine her, digging out juicy bits of gossip to take back.*

'Matthee Weeks of course. Who else did such a terrible thing to the poor maid? Isaac Cory told me himself he'd seen Weeks walking with a woman on the moors the very day she went missing.'

''Tis true Cory said so. I heard 'en say he noticed the woman wearing a red shawl. Us do all know Charlotte wore a red shawl to chapel Sundays. 'Twas foggy, Cory said.'

William Northam stopped talking, as if thinking, and scratched his head.

''Tis strange then to be so certain, if 'twas foggy. But Isaac said 'twas easy to recognise Weeks clearly, because he walked with a twist.'

'Funny then how Cory didn't recognise poor Charlotte in her scarlet shawl,' a*n unknown man's voice said, with a snort of derision.*

'He said to me at the cattle market he weren't sure which maid 'twas in that fog below Roughtor. But he were damn sure 'twas Matthee Weeks out there, up to no good.'

He paused.

'Cory always did hate Matthee, mind, ever since they quarrelled over some missing bullocks a few years back.'

The cart jolted in a deep rut. I wanted to cry out to them all that Matthew had nothing to do with my death. He even hated killing the pigs on the farm, he could not bear the squealing and the gush of blood as he slit their throats. I knew Matthew wouldn't have harmed a hair on my head, for all I made him jealous with my flirting and foolish talk. We had quarrelled on our walk that Sunday afternoon, mostly about a silly letter, which he could not read. And then we had gone our separate ways. I had told Matthew that Mrs Peter had given me notice to quit the farm, but looking back I believe he thought I just wanted to get away from him. The letter was about a place on a farm at Blisland where I could find work, I said. He was angry at first and some upset with me. We had strong words at Roughtor ford, and then I walked off alone. The last thing I remember about Matthew was his voice, shouting desperately through the mist, telling me not to go. He shouted that he loved me, and no one, not even Tommy Prout, could love me more than him. And I, like a fool, ignored his pleadings and kept on walking, picking my way through the marshy ground in my pattens.

'Twas not Matthew Weeks, who slit my naked neck at Roughtor, for all their say-so.

When the cart carrying my body rumbled into the farmyard, Mistress Peter and her son John were waiting.

''Tis a sorry procession, Missus,' *said a deep voice I knew well ('twas that of Simon Baker from Trevalga),* 'bringing an innocent maid home like this.'

'You didn't call her an innocent maid when she wouldn't stop laughing in chapel and the Minister called her a whore after,' *said a man's gruff voice in a low tone.*

'Shush now! Poor Charlotte is dead and gone.'

'Twas my Mistress's voice, as sharp as a knife.

'Show some respect for the maid now that she has come back home to Penhale.'

The cart jolted again.

'Hold the harness, John.'

'Take her body to rest in the barn.'

'In the barn, mother?'

Mary Westlake had the temerity to question her mother.

'In the barn, Mary.'

Mrs Peter's voice was firm.

'Thomas Good, the surgeon from Lewannick will be coming here tomorrow. He has to view poor Charlotte's body, before he can make his report.'

And so I was carried into the stone barn by the menfolk. They laid me on the same trestle table we'd use for harvest supper. I almost laughed to think of my poor body being laid out where the cold meats, proper harvest fare and jugs of cider always stood. The Mistress straightened my gown out to look respectable and stood over me, looking closely at the awful wound on my neck.

'Who do 'e think would have done such a terrible thing?' *her daughter said in a loud whisper.*

'Matthee Weeks may be able to tell us more,' *Mrs. Peter said bluntly, as she looked down at my body,* 'when he be found that is. 'Tis looking black for Matthee. But for now, we must be seen to do right by this maid. The neighbours be all talking nineteen to the dozen as 'tis. We have to think of our position, Mary. The whole parish'll be here, nosing, afore we know it.'

She laid a weathered hand on my tangled hair and in a softer tone she said: 'Charlotte's mother never even wanted her. No father, of course. Couldn't wait to get her in service, they say. 'Tis even rumoured that she threatened to kill the maid herself. May Charlotte rest in peace now, with the Lord.'

And they went out and left me lying there, alone. No lit candles, no one to mourn my loss; just the scuffling of mice in the hay and the fading shafts of April light slanting through the cracks in the wooden shutter across the barn window.

TWENTY NINE

IT was a bright, but cold morning. The sun was filtering through a gap in the heavy curtains. Poppy woke in her untidy bed by the ashes of the fire. Winston was treading the covers, purring loudly. In barely an hour, her car was making its way up the lane, towards the main road. Everything was glittering with frost. She reached the junction and stopped dead. Which way? Should she take the road that led to Launceston? Or should she turn left and trek towards Camelford and then on to Bodmin? Decisions, decisions. Her day would be totally different if she went to Bodmin, for she knew she would want to follow up her previous visit to the old gaol in some way. If she headed to Launceston she would feel obliged to call in at Annie's place and maybe get in touch with Josh on the way back.

Her mobile bleeped with a text. Josh. How weird that she had been thinking of him at that very moment. Still sitting at the junction, she read his text. Josh had been injured in a rugby tackle at Polson. Nothing broken, just a bad sprain, but it was painful. He wasn't working today. What was she up to? She sent a brief reply and shoved her mobile into her bag. She indicated right and turned on to the Launceston road, heading in the direction of St Clether.

'O sad Saint Clether' came into her mind as the sun glinted on the smeared windscreen, making driving difficult. The words were from a poem by Thomas Hardy, one she'd read at college years ago. One summer they had embarked on a Hardy Pilgrimage to St Clether and Boscastle. They were supposed to finish their outing at Beeny, on the high cliffs, but the weather had been against them that day. She remembered sheltering from the rain in the damp church porch at St Clether and having a picnic there instead.

Hardy had visited St Clether in a pony and trap from St Juliot, with Emma Gifford who was later to become his wife. Emma wanted to call in at the vicarage to see the vicar's sick son. The man had apparently wanted to marry Emma himself. The green-eyed god of jealousy must have been with Thomas Hardy that day, for he had done something unforgiveable. When the white face of the dying young man appeared at the upper window of the vicarage, Hardy had put his arm around Emma as if to say: 'She is mine, you have lost her.'

And now Poppy was driving towards St Clether where the pony and trap had gone before, and the poor young man had been lying in his grave in the churchyard for long, long years.

'If she won't have me, I'll make sure no one else does.'

Words uttered out of jealousy and bitterness came suddenly to Poppy. Words supposedly spoken by Matthew Weeks, some fifty or so years before Thomas Hardy's visit to Cornwall. Damning words, from the testimony of Isaac Cory, the man on the moor with malice in his eyes. The uncle of Tommy Prout, no less, who had visited Charlotte on the morning of her last Sunday at Penhale Farm.

A rabbit bolted in front of the car and Poppy braked hard, her heart pounding. She knew she had been distracted from driving. She scrambled out of the car quickly and found the poor creature lying in the ditch. Her eyes filled with tears of self-recrimination and pity. As she knelt to inspect it, the dazed rabbit recovered and in a sudden burst of desperate energy it hurtled through a gap in the hedge to freedom. What was she doing, she asked herself, so absorbed with her muddled thoughts of the past that she was not even watching the road? She climbed back into the car and switched on the radio. The gentle voice of Cat Stevens, softly singing, appropriately, *Morning Has Broken*.

The corners of her mouth turned up in a small smile as her car bumped along the narrow lane leading to Josh's farm. What sort of welcome would she get, she wondered. Josh's mother was always studiously polite, but there was an edge there, she knew. His parents certainly did not approve of an unstable, would-be artist having such a close relationship with their beloved eldest son. No doubt they would like Josh to meet a farmer's daughter, with acres of fertile farmland and a range of outbuildings and tumbledown barns.

Barns, in various stages of conversion, were the first buildings she saw as she drove into the yard. Timber, stone and bags of cement were piled up against one wall. A dog was barking loudly, announcing her arrival. A face appeared at a top window. Josh, unusually pale, was wearing an expression of disbelief when he realised who was in the yard.

'All I need now is for a young farmer to come and put his arm around me while Josh is watching, and history will have repeated itself here at St Clether,' she mused, as she gathered her bag.

'Morning!'

Josh's father, John, emerged from a barn, his farmer's cap pulled well down over his eyes.

'You'd best come on in out of the cold. The kitchen will be warm enough, but Josh is still in bed, I reckon.'

He stomped on ahead of her towards the back door in his filthy boots.

'He got injured at rugby last night. Nothing too bad, but it's another day working short-handed.'

Poppy followed on behind him into the back porch, with its usual jumble of coats, wellies and sticks. The farmhouse kitchen was warm and welcoming, if somewhat old-fashioned. There was an appetising smell of bacon and mushrooms frying. Josh's mother looked back over her shoulder from the Rayburn. Her face did not flicker when she saw Poppy behind her husband in the doorway.

'Oh, hello Poppy. I didn't know you were here. Grab a seat at the table. You will join us for some breakfast, won't you?'

She glanced at her husband.

'John has been up for hours loading bullocks for the market. Don't go thinking we usually eat at this late hour.'

Poppy sat at the scrubbed table, making polite yet stilted conversation with Josh's mother. She wished Josh would hurry up and come downstairs. John, was already scrubbing his hands at the kitchen sink, cap still firmly on his head. He glanced back over his shoulder at Poppy.

'Where is that boy to?'

The scene was strangely familiar, somehow. The empty staircase in the corner. The shrewd-eyed woman of about sixty or so. The man scrubbing his filthy hands at the sink. For a moment Poppy almost felt she was back in the kitchen of the farm at Penhale, with Mrs Peter asking her servants about the missing farmhand.

A footstep on the stair made her turn gratefully towards the sound. A young man hobbled into view.

'Matthew?'

Her voice was strange, not her own. There was a moment when time seemed to slow. She was vaguely aware of the curious stare of the grey-haired woman, pausing in her task of frying. The man at the sink turned with a concerned expression on his face, his arms dripping with soapy water. The young man emerged from the shadowy corner by the stairs, crippling on a painful leg…

'Josh.'

His father's low voice spoke with a degree of urgency.

'What's taken you so long?'

He faced his son, towelling his hands and arms roughly.

'My leg's bloody killing me, that's why.'

Josh immediately took in the whole tense scene: Poppy's white face and shaking hands, his father's grim expression, his mother's stiff back, as she dished generous portions on to hot plates.

'Hi Poppy. Saw you from the window.'

He slumped clumsily next to her at the table.

'Great you're here to join us for some breakfast. I keep telling mum you're in need of a good feed.'

The awkward moment was broken. Gradually some sense of normality returned to the kitchen. Josh's father, John, droned on to him between mouthfuls about bad tackles and rugby injuries, while his mother made quiet small-talk with Poppy, mostly about how her mother was getting on in America. The subject of Matt's death was avoided. It was obviously taboo, she thought. But who could blame them? What more was there to say?

'So what shall we do today? Now that I can't work, we might as well go somewhere or do something.'

Josh avoided his father's hard stare and smiled at Poppy.

'As long as it's not too much walking, I'm happy.'

Josh's mother started to pick up the greasy plates with a clatter.

'You've hardly touched your food, Poppy. You really ought to eat more to get your strength up.'

'Leave the girl alone, Sarah,' said John as he got up from the table. 'I'm sure she's old enough to know whether she's hungry or not.'

Poppy smiled at him gratefully and picked up her plate of unfinished bacon and Josh's plate that he'd wiped clean with a piece of bread.

'Now where did the paper go?'

Josh picked up a crumpled newspaper from where he'd been sitting on it. He smoothed it out and slung it on the table towards his father.

An unearthly cry from the depths of Poppy made them all freeze. She had picked up the newspaper in trembling hands. Its headline was clear to see: *Ice picnickers condemned.* But it was the disturbing photograph that had struck such a chilling chord with her. It showed a frozen reservoir below Roughtor and Brown Willy. On the ice was a wrought iron table, with a red cloth, a bottle of wine and two filled glasses. Two metal chairs stood ready and waiting for a couple to dine on the ice.

'I was there last night, with Matt,' she whispered hoarsely, gasping for breath.

She held out the photograph towards Josh.

'I was there and the ice was cracking beneath my feet.'

Thirty

TIME is a strange but wonderful thing. It is an enigma. Sometimes there is just not enough of it. Like when someone you love is dying and all time is precious. Then there are other days when time hangs heavy on your hands, like on a hot oppressive day, and it slows almost to a stop. It was nearly quarter of an hour since Poppy's outburst in the farmhouse kitchen. It had been a long and difficult time for them all.

Josh's father, just like so many other men, coughed in an embarrassed sort of way, pulled on his boots and made his escape as soon as possible to get away. He could immerse himself in his work, happy to be away from the drama being played out in his own kitchen. Anyway, he had to be at the livestock market at Hallworthy before too long.

It was not so easy for Sarah, Josh's mother. She did not like the girl, but her maternal feelings took over and she wanted to give Poppy comfort of sorts. Her own mother was nothing short of useless, if what Josh had to say about her was true. It was obvious the girl had mental problems, and physically she looked so thin and wrung out. But for all that, she did not like the way her son was getting drawn into the role of supporting Poppy, with all its pressures. As if on cue, Josh was holding the girl in his arms, stroking her hair tenderly, kissing her bowed head. Sarah cleared her throat to speak.

'When you say you were with Matt last night, what do you mean exactly?'

She swallowed hard.

'I know it is hard for you to accept, Poppy, but Matt is dead. You are still grieving for his loss. It makes people behave in all sorts of different ways. Perhaps it was just a bad dream you had last night.'

Josh scowled at his mother over the top of Poppy's head.

'I was there, on the ice.'

Her low voice was muffled, yet insistent.

'My feet were freezing cold. There was a table, just like that photo on the front page of the newspaper; there were two wine glasses, filled with red wine. Matt kept calling to me, to cross the icy surface to be with him.'

Sarah raised her eyebrows at her son and shrugged her shoulders awkwardly. She was at a loss to know what to do or say.

'Shall I make you a nice cup of tea with lots of sugar? It might make you feel a bit better, love.'

'Why is it that a cup of tea is always the answer to every bleddy thing?' Josh yelled.

'Don't, Josh.'

Poppy raised her white face from the comfort of his solid chest.

'Your mum is only trying to help.'

Stung by her son's attack, Sarah turned her back. She stared out of the window and then switched on the kettle. She tucked strands of greying hair behind her ears and turned her attention to the pile of dishes waiting to be washed. Soon the clattering of cutlery and crockery filled the kitchen.

'Let's go somewhere. Anywhere,' Josh whispered.

Poppy nodded.

The rays of sunlight made the hedges and trees sparkle as they drove out of the farmyard. Josh's father watched them go from the doorway of the largest barn, frowning under his cap. He scratched his head and made his way back to the house now that the coast was clear. Thank God that his younger son, Tom, was not involved with a headcase like that Poppy, he thought.

It was Josh who broke the silence in the car.

'It's the moors, you know. They seem to have such a strange effect on you.'

'But the moors are so beautiful,' Poppy said softly. 'I love their sense of mystery. I love their loneliness when I hear the wind whistling around the rocks.'

She drove slowly through the high-sided meandering lanes. Josh was cramped in the passenger seat, his leg giving him considerable pain.

'But they make you behave so strangely. As if you see ghosts every bloody where you look, Poppy.'

She managed a small smile as she changed down a gear before a particularly dangerous bend.

'Well there is a timeless quality about the moors. Surely you must be able to feel it too? When you are on the top of the tors surrounded by incredibly strange-shaped stones, with the wind blowing in your face?'

Josh shifted in his seat and made an inarticulate sound in reply. Poppy slowed to a grinding halt in an open gateway.

'I am just so embarrassed about what happened in front of your parents in your kitchen.'

She reached for her bag with its tin of ready-rolled cigarettes.

'I am truly sorry, Josh. If they disliked me before, they must really hate me now.'

She looked straight into his eyes.

'Hate is a very strong word,' he said with a wry grin. 'They just worry about me, that's all. They think I'm under your spell.'

'And are you under my spell?'

She lit her cigarette and offered one to Josh.

'You make me sound like one of the wise women of the olden days. You know what I mean, someone at one with Nature, who instinctively sees ghosts and beasts at every turn. God knows I would probably have been taken for a witch, living alone in such an isolated cottage with only a black cat for company.'

'Come on Poppy, you know I am under your fricking spell. Have been for years. But all this stuff with ghosts and shadows and supernatural smells is frightening you to bloody death. And I'm not too keen on it myself, come to that.'

He lit his cigarette, snapped his lighter shut and lifted his leg into a less painful position in the cramped foot well.

'Strangely enough, I am not so frightened any more.'

Her green eyes were glittering in the sunlight.

'But there are so many things happening to me that are totally inexplicable; like that news article in today's local paper. I mean, how did that surreal story of the dinner table on the icy reservoir get into print, when I only experienced it last night? And why was Matt there, calling to me across the ice when it was cracking all around me? There are so many questions that need answering.'

She blew smoke out of the car window and frowned hard as she remembered.

'On top of all that, why were the beads of Charlotte Dymond's necklace scattered on the ice under the table, like beads of blood?'

Silence prevailed for a few minutes.

'We could go to Davidstow and look for her grave if you like.'

Josh could hardly believe he was saying this.

'Did you know that every year someone still puts fresh flowers on Charlotte's grave, on her anniversary?'

Poppy's green eyes widened at this tangible mystery. She started the car and crushed the remains of her cigarette in the ash-tray.

Davidstow Church lies in a dip in the main road between Launceston and Camelford. They arrived to find rooks wheeling around their nests in the tall trees, cawing above the peace and quiet of the churchyard. Josh was limping badly as they made their way up the path.

'Charlotte's grave is marked by a broken cross. I read somewhere it was taken from the church roof during renovations absolutely years ago.'

Poppy's eyes were keenly scanning the older headstones, many of them covered with lichen and soft silky moss.

'Look, you know I'll stand by you on this crazy search of yours, wherever it leads you.' Josh hesitated before he continued. 'But I won't bloody well let dabbling in the past destroy you.'

Charlotte felt very close at hand now. Poppy stood still. She could only begin to imagine Charlotte's funeral, an illegitimate girl, dropped into her grave with no parents to weep over her...

'It's here,' she said and knelt instinctively, sweeping long grass away from a broken cross near the path. 'I know it. It's Charlotte's grave.'

THIRTY ONE

*They said my burial at Davidstow was a heart-rending
sight. They said at the graveside I was 'the fruit of an
illicit love'. Some said I was spurned from the door of my
mother who was 'in nature' bound to protect me. The
curate, John Gillard, did not even give me a proper
church funeral service. Perhaps my life and death were
so much more to do with the work of the devil that the
church could not, or would not, allow my mutilated body
to enter its holy portals. However it was John Gillard's
own hand that wrote the entry in the burial register. It
read: Charlotte Dymond, Penhale, April 25th 1844, aged
19 years.*

*I had rested, as they called it, in the barn at Penhale
Farm for three days. 'Twas right and proper, they said,
for 'twas the place where I had lived and worked.
Penhale was where I had milked the cows until my hands
were red and my back ached. 'Twas also where I helped
my mistress in the farmhouse, with the heavier house-
work and in the dairy.*

*The work at Penhale was hard, but I was in service
and expected nothing different. My early childhood had
been hard and bitter, with a mother who could not abide
me... I can remember the look in her eyes. Eyes as hard
as pebbles. I never had one kind word from that woman.
I was the living embodiment of her shame and she could
not wait to get rid of me.*

*'I wish that you were dead,' she would hiss at me
often, when my childish hands, outstretched like starfish,
would seek comfort from her. My tears would flow but*

her heart was hardened against me from the moment of my birth. Even in the darkness of her womb she loathed me.

My mother was not at my funeral, nor did I wish her to be. I remember once overhearing Elias Bettison of Davidstow saying I was a poor friendless creature, the bastard child from Boscastle and that my mother was against me. And so I had been sent away early, to work in service at Penhale Farm at the tender age of eleven years. 'Twas rumoured, Elias had said, that rather than I should come inside her door ever again that my mother would kill me.

And my father? I never knew who my father was, though there were whisperings. Sometimes I would look at the men leaning over the rails looking at the cattle at the livestock market, when I accompanied the mistress. I would make up stories about one of them. I would pick out a handsome man of course to be my secret father, someone with kind eyes and a smile. One day he would come to Penhale to find me and call me his own pretty maid and tell me how much he had always loved me. But that day never came.

The only one to ever say he truly loved me was Matthew Weeks. Poor Matthew, with his lame leg and his pock-marked face. He tried hard to make up for his lack of handsome looks by dressing in fancy clothes. But despite all this and his shame that he could neither read nor write, he had a good, kind heart. All Matthew ever wanted was to look after me, just like he looked after my best clothes in a box in his bedroom at Penhale.

And now Matthew was lying in a dark cell in the grim gaol at Bodmin, waiting for his trial for my murder. And I was observing my own funeral at Davidstow.

When the procession got ready to leave Penhale farm with my coffin to move towards Davidstow churchtown, they all sang a hymn. I was amazed at the number of folk gathered there. 'Twas a send-off not to be missed, that much was clear. Deep black and solemn mourning was the order of the day.

My mistress, Mrs Peter, the chief mourner, was all black bonnet and feathers, her black jet beads winking on her best high-necked blouse. Her unmarried son John stood next to her, studying the toes of his polished boots. Soft he was, all of us knew it. No woman would look at soft John Peter, ruled as he was with a rod of iron by his mother. John Stevens, who worked with us at Penhale, used to laugh at him behind his back.

Yet there was no laughter to be seen on John Stevens' face today. He looked scrubbed and clean. But was that a tear in his eye? He had shared a bedroom with poor Matthew; as servants they had to sleep together in a room with John Peter, who had his own bed. Had Matthew shared his secret thoughts and dreams about me with John Stevens, while soft John Peter snored the dreamless nights away?

Mary Westlake, my mistress's gossipy daughter, was relishing the occasion. With a new black gown and bonnet to show off in her important role as mourner and masses of parish folk to see her near the head of the procession, what more could she want? There was such little excitement and life was generally hard, so she was determined to enjoy the day. Her button eyes darted around the assembled crowd, watching everyone and everything closely, for she would feed off this day for years to come. Her hen-pecked husband stood dutifully by her side, twisting a black hat in his hands.

I did not know the hymn they were singing, for we usually went to the chapel at Tremail and 'twas very different hymns sung there.

On one occasion in chapel, I remember, the minister

turned on me when he believed I had been laughing out loud during the service. I was mortified when he called me all sorts of terrible names... but there was a thrill in it for all that! I remember Tommy Prout staring at me that morning across the pews with a mixture of admiration and lust in his handsome dark eyes.

I could not see Tommy Prout amongst the huge crowd, but I could see Tommy's horrible uncle, Isaac Cory from Trevilian's Gate. All of us young girls disliked him for his lecherous eyes and his sweating hands. There he stood in his chapel clothes with his thinning hair wetted and slicked back, next to his fat wife in her voluminous gown and rusty bonnet, looking important for all the parish to see. After all, Cory was a proper land-owner now. And, not that you could believe a word he ever said, a witness in the true story of my murder.

'Strange how Isaac Cory visited the place where Charlotte's body was found near Roughtor ford and immediately found her missing bits and pieces in a turfy pit!' I was aware of a woman's loud whisper somewhere on the edge of the crowd. 'Constable Rickard saw him out on the marsh with his wife. He saw them pull something from a pit.' Her friend nodded, and after a dramatic pause she added: ''Twas a single shoe. Then a patten, then another shoe. 'Twas followed by a soaking-wet red shawl and a silk bonnet.'

The procession moved off slowly along the lane, my coffin lurching as they went across the fields and out on to the road. Another hymn was sung, near where Chapman the butcher lived, and then they all carried on towards Tremail.

'I'll meet you at Tremail, Charlotte.' Tommy's words came back to me, and he had kissed me then, his breath as sweet as honey. I remembered his laughing, handsome face close to mine and how my heart had thudded so, I thought he could hear it. His touch on my arm had made me shiver in my best Sunday gown and petticoats as he helped me through the deep mud of the lane. His kisses and embraces were the undoing of me.

So 'twas at Tremail, the very place where I had arranged to meet Tommy on the evening I disappeared from Penhale, that the last hymn was sung. The words had been written by someone in the parish, 'twas said, about the sad story of my short life.

Dear friends, behold a helpless child
Left thoughtless, giddy, young and wild,
In childhood banished from her home,
Nor near her parents durst she come.

Well, who would have thought it? A special hymn written for me, a lowly milkmaid. It made me laugh triumphantly to see them singing my hymn, some with tears flowing down their cheeks; all those same holier-than-thou people who had looked down their noses at me in Tremail Chapel when the Minister called me a disgrace for my bubbling laughter during the service. Now I was enjoying myself.

So why were these same stiff-necked people, so affected by my sudden death? Was it the violence of the attack on me? Or did they feel remorse and guilt for their own cruel treatment of me, a poor bastard child from Boscastle with no one to love and protect me? After all, I was an innocent maiden who had worked my fingers to the bone for my mistress on the farm. The horror of my end must have touched their consciences, these chapel and church folk.

And, I asked myself, who had paid for this grand funeral?

The procession moved sluggishly on its way from

Tremail towards Davidstow church. All along the wayside, more people were standing silently in cottage doorways. Children were shushed as my coffin passed by, followed by the solemn line of mourners and sympathisers. Some of the women looked like old crows in their dusty black and feathers, I thought, and it gave me much merriment as I watched them, their black wings of shawls flapping in the April breeze.

And so, at last, the procession came to the plot in the churchyard, south of the church. 'Twas near the pathway, I noticed, so that my grave would be seen and my story remembered for years to come. Rooks were cawing loudly in the tall trees and the wind blew the spring grass of the churchyard.

The people crowded near for a sight of the proceedings. I felt a mixture of emotions as I watched the coffin drop into the cold earth, for 'twas my coffin, and my mutilated body lay inside it.

The curate prayed over the gaping hole. The crowds gathered around, jostling near the graveside, desperate for one last look at the coffin of a murdered girl.

I saw my mistress, Mrs Peter, with a strange look on her face as she stared into the pit. I remembered her words to her daughter Mary Westlake, when my body was laid in the barn at Penhale. 'The whole parish will be nosing into our affairs afore too long. We must be seen to do right by this maid.' The curate prayed in a loud voice so all could hear, that Charlotte Dymond, an innocent young woman who had met her death so violently and so tragically, would soon meet her Lord face-to-face. He finished with a flourish. 'May she rest in peace for all eternity.'

The people gradually moved away from the churchyard, leaving the sexton to fill in the grave with shovelfuls of rich-smelling brown earth. The last few *primroses in the hedgerows blew gently in the soft breeze and a blackbird sang from a nearby hedge. 'Twas a peaceful place to rest in.*

But I knew that my spirit would never rest. I would never sleep peacefully in the quiet earth. I would haunt the moors and the places I loved, but I would not rest. Not 'til the true story of my untimely death was revealed.

THIRTY TWO

THE visit to Charlotte's grave had churned up Poppy's feelings once more. She knelt in the long grass for some time, sensing the echoes of the tragedy surrounding the long-dead girl. The knees of her jeans were wet but she was unaware of the discomfort. She ran her fingertips over the stone of the broken cross, feeling its rough surface.

'If only stones could speak,' she whispered, her voice cracking with emotion.

'Some people reckon they can.'

Josh's deep voice behind her came as a surprise, jolting her. In the intensity of the moment she had almost forgotten he was there with her, in Davidstow churchyard. She looked up at him, amazed at his response. After all this was down-to-earth Josh speaking.

'I read in a book that a growing number of people believe there is a link between ghosts and stone. Just think of the moors, Poppy. There is so much stone everywhere, so is it any wonder they're said to be haunted?'

He squatted next to her in the grass, then the pain in his leg shot up through his body making him get up with some alacrity. The pain seared through his brain, like a knife.

'Shit! I forgot about my bloody leg.'

Poppy got up to support him. He was biting his lip so hard between his teeth that he had drawn blood. He leaned on her briefly, standing on one leg, his face twisted with pain. Josh's expression gradually assumed its usual friendly grin and he attempted to pitch some weight on his foot before hobbling a step or two down the path.

'See? I can cripple back to the car if you're nearly ready.'

Poppy watched him lurch down the path, putting most of his weight on his good leg. A voice from the past pushed into her brain.

'I think 'twas Matthee Weeks I saw by Roughtor Ford that day.'Twas his way of walking, see. He dipped a mite in walking. He walked like a lame man...'

Josh was not a lame man. But today he was walking like one. Could someone else have pretended to walk like Matthee Weeks on the moor that day back in 1844? If the light was poor and the watchers were far off, might it not have been an easy mistake to assume the man was Matthew? Poppy took one last lingering look at the grave with its broken cross and said softly: 'I wish you could lead me to the truth about your death, Charlotte... then you could sleep well at last.'

Deep in her own thoughts, she followed the churchyard path down to the gateway. Josh was limping ahead of her, his head down and shoulders rumped up. Slowly he turned to face her. She was aware of the noise of the rooks and the wind seemed to blow more coldly. The sky darkened ominously to an inky black over the church tower.

It was not Josh who was standing before her on the path with a solemn look on his face. But she recognised the man easily. It was Tommy Prout, a ghost in time, dressed in funereal black. He brushed past her without seeing her there on the path and made his way to Charlotte's grave. It was a new grave. There was no lichen-covered cross to mark the spot. The flowers were fresh and the rich earth was newly dug. Tommy stood in front of the grave in silent thought. The wind blew across the churchyard and he swept his dark hair back from his eyes in an action that seemed somehow familiar.

What were the thoughts going through his mind as he gazed at Charlotte's newly-dug grave? Those dark flashing eyes, which had laughed and flirted with the living girl out on the moor and in the country lanes, were now fixed on the fresh earth. He stood there in contemplation for some time. Suddenly he squatted down on his haunches and gently touched the delicate petals of the spring flowers laid there. It was as if he was searching for something... something tangible, now that all the crowds of people had feasted their eyes and gone home with their gossip and tales to tell of a funeral not to be forgotten in Cornwall.

He spoke in a low voice, so low that Poppy could not hear him, all the time stroking the petals with his fingers as one might caress the skin of a lover. What was Tommy Prout saying? Was he speaking to Charlotte, now cold and dead, buried six feet deep? Was he remembering the touch of her skin, the taste of her kisses? Was he thinking of her blushes as she had picked up her petticoats out of the mud, showing her trim ankles in black stockings? After all, he had been captivated by Charlotte, the pretty milkmaid from Penhale with the red lips and the flirtatious manner. He had enjoyed time spent with her, they'd had fun on their country walks, teasing each other, leading each other on with sweet kisses and talk. Even better, if it made that miserable Matthee Weeks jealous.

Like that time Weeks had caught them laughing together in the yard at Penhale after she had finished the milking. Her simple clothes had enhanced her beautiful face, framed by the tendrils of her black hair that had escaped from her milkmaid's cap. There was a sweetness about her that was irresistible. How Matthew had scowled at them both that day as he'd emerged from the mowhay at the back of the farmhouse, stick in hand.

Tommy had once worked with Matthew, like his uncle Isaac Cory had done before him, and they had not got on. He announced to Matthew that very morning when he had come upon him in the meadow at the back that he was thinking of moving to live and work at Penhale. He was getting tired of living at Lesnewth, some four miles off, he'd said, in a casual tone. Tommy had grinned then, his handsome face lighting up as he saw Matthew's expression become even more sullen than usual.

'If I decide to move to Penhale, Matthee, you had better look out for your girlfriend. I reckon I shall be depriving you of her, afore long.'

Tommy had laughed then, loud and long and continued to goad Weeks, enjoying the farmhand's obvious discomfort. Voices were soon raised between the two young men, for John Stevens the servant had later remembered Matthew shouting: 'If you move to Penhale to work, Prout, then I shall move out. Us'll never agree living in the same place, for so 'twas when we lived together last time.'

More goading from Tommy Prout had been followed by a torrent of abuse from Weeks, before he walked off in anger. He was already smouldering when he later caught sight of Charlotte in fits of girlish laughter with Tommy in the farmyard. She was leaning back in a relaxed way against the shippen wall, a milking stool in her hand. The sunlight was glinting on the shiny blue-black strands of her hair and her red mouth was laughing at some amusing little thing that had just been said. And now that mouth would laugh no more. And the pretty maid was lying under the cold Davidstow earth, whispering: 'Remember me...'

Tommy Prout stood up stiffly. He brushed some grass from his trousers, unaware that another man was walking quietly up the path behind him.

Isaac Cory, for it was his uncle, spoke in an urgent, angry tone.

'What be 'e doing here, boy? You should know better 'n to be out here on your own.'

Tommy's eyes misted up.

'Folks'll talk, Tommy, if you'm seen here at Charlotte's grave, all on your own.'

Cory glanced around nervously, as if they might be being watched.

'Come on now, time to be getting back homewards.'

Poppy watched the older man pull on his nephew's arm and lead him down the pathway. They walked past her, unaware of her presence, to the church gate where she could see Cory's pony and trap waiting.

Feeling stunned and confused, she followed in the men's wake. One hand on the wooden gate, she paused. The pony and trap had disappeared. There in its place was her car, parked in the lay-by under the trees. She could see Josh dozing inside it, his head resting against the window.

High, high above, she could hear a skylark singing and the sound of the wind blowing from the moors.

THIRTY THREE

POPPY watched as Josh hobbled into the farmhouse, turning to wave at the granite doorway. He probably needed to see a doctor, but he was always so damnably stubborn. His leg would mend on its own, he'd said. Josh's father was still at Hallworthy market, probably in the pub, and it was his mother's afternoon for Patchwork in some church hall or other, so thankfully Poppy was spared the embarrassment of seeing them again so soon after her dramatic outburst earlier.

That evening she got out her neglected sketch-book and produced some charcoal drawings of Winston. She looked at them critically: Winston washing himself, one leg extended; Winston curled up, sleeping; Winston sitting up, sphinx-like. It had been weeks since she had painted or sketched, but there was some merit to be seen in the cat drawings, which made her feel almost happy. Her artistic talent had not deserted her then. As she sketched, she formed a plan. She would go to Boscastle again to visit Gweniver. Perhaps she would be more forthcoming about Charlotte Dymond without her grandson present.

The following morning Gweniver opened the door to her white-washed cottage with the words: 'I've been expecting you, maid. Knew you'd be back to see me some time or other! You'd best come in.'

Poppy automatically bent her head as she entered under a horse-shoe nailed to the lintel. She followed the bent-backed woman into the cluttered kitchen. It smelled, as she remembered, of baking. This time it was the warm, friendly smell of bread. Gweniver motioned to Poppy to sit, as she cleared a saggy armchair of an elderly tabby cat with hostile eyes and a voluminous purple knitting bag with needles sticking out of it precariously. She put the kettle on and turned to face Poppy. Gweniver's face was a bit like a brown, wrinkled walnut, thought Poppy. But for all that, her eyes were as bright and alive as a monkey's.

'So what can I do for you then maid? My Josh not with you today then.'

Her monkey eyes lit up at the mention of her favourite grandson.

'He got injured at rugby.'

Poppy saw the concern in the old woman's expression, and added hastily: 'But it's nothing serious! It's just he's not out and about so much at the moment.'

'That darned old rugby. Worries me sick when I see them tackles they do. But you can't wrap 'em in cotton wool I always say.'

Gweniver turned to her blackened teapot and found some clean cups near the crowded sink. Her wispy, silver hair was escaping from its many clips and combs.

'It's Charlotte Dymond you want to talk about, I feel.'

She poured boiling water into the pot, then she faced Poppy once more.

'Am I right?'

'How did you know?'

Poppy was amazed. Josh had jokingly mentioned his gran could almost be one of the infamous Boscastle witches. Now it seemed a distinct possibility.

'You'd be surprised what I know,' said Gweniver, pouring boiling water into the pot, steam misting up the kitchen window.

'There's folk in Boscastle think I'm a bit mad, you

know. Because I see things, things that others don't. Like ghosts, and beasts too.'

She handed a rose-patterned cup of tea to Poppy with her claw-like hand, covered with brown age-spots.

'So I keep most of it to myself, you could say.'

She pursed up her lips to blow the tea.

'But one thing I do know, that Charlotte's ghost has been seen by many people over the years.'

She nodded vehemently and looked at Poppy with her bright monkey eyes.

'I've seen her,' Poppy blurted. 'Out on the moor. More than once.'

'I thought as much, maid. Well, you said as much when you visited before. Something about her coming to you one evening, her face at the window.'

'Yes.'

She hesitated for a moment.

'It scared me to death the first time she made contact with me at Penhale Cottage, but now... now I don't feel so scared any more. It's as if I've got a growing bond with Charlotte. I'm beginning to understand why she won't rest.'

The old woman nodded again, understandingly.

'She had a hard time, Charlotte Dymond. Poor maid.'

She sighed deeply.

'The Bastard of Boscastle, some folk cruelly called her. Not that she was the only one by any means. But as I always say, 'twas different days back then. Charlotte's mother thought she was too good for the likes of many around here. Well she had learning, see. Teacher, with her nose up in the air. But her was just like all the rest, underneath her fine clothes. A good-looking man was her undoing, and an unwanted child, little Charlotte, was the result of that.'

Poppy felt icily cold suddenly, as if an arctic blast had passed through the steamy kitchen. Gweniver looked at her shrewdly.

'Something wrong maid? 'Tis crystal-clear to me, that you can sense things too.'

'It's nothing.'

Poppy shook her head.

'Just a sudden coldness, as if someone was walking over my grave.'

The old woman put her cup down.

'I knew instinctively when you came here with my Joshua that you were different to the others. I can read a character you know. Some folk in Boscastle think I can read their minds and all.'

She laughed, in a creaky voice.

'P'raps they worry that I can see all their little wrong-doings.'

She watched the girl closely, noting her thin, wasted body and abundance of wild red hair.

'Sometimes I feel that there is someone in the room with me, but there is no one there. Then perhaps I see a figure, just passing through, but no one else can see it. So I usually keep quiet about it.'

Poppy twisted her long, silk scarf in her fingers as she spoke.

'My friends already think I am pretty unstable, so it's easier to keep some things to myself at times.'

Gweniver nodded in agreement. Silence prevailed for a short time, only the loud ticking of an ancient clock could be heard and the wheezy breathing of the old cat, sleeping in a patch of sunlight by the back door.

'They say that the ghost of Charlotte was seen crossing the moor several times years ago when they had camps of Rifle Volunteers in the Roughtor area, you know.'

Poppy lifted her head, curious to hear more.

'The men hated doing night-time guard duty. There were always arguments, they say, for many were too scared to be posted out there, alone in the dark. They came back terrified, saying they had seen the ghost of a woman, wearing a bonnet and old-fashioned clothes.'

Gweniver took a deep, rasping breath and continued quietly.

'You'll find there is a lot of psychic activity out on the moor at Roughtor. 'Tis haunted by more ghosts 'n Charlotte Dymond. But then, the strange stones invite unseen presences out there. I reckon 'tis just the same at places like the Cheesewring, out at Minions. And you've got stone circles out there too, maid.'

The old woman's eyes were far, far away. Perhaps in another time, even. Poppy was afraid to move or make a sound, wrapped in her own thoughts. The clock ticked on loudly. In the tiny kitchen window, some hanging crystals reflected the light in rainbow colours and tinkled in an unseen breeze. She felt relaxed here, in Josh's gran's tiny white-washed cottage with its abundance of spring flowers gently blowing out in the garden. She felt accepted.

Half-an-hour later, she was driving back down through the village. On the passenger seat next to her was a small loaf of newly-baked bread, still warm from Gweniver's oven.

THIRTY FOUR

SHE woke up that night, in a sweat about Matt. She could hear him playing his guitar softly in her dreams. His face kept coming to her, with those amazing eyes fixed on hers. His expression was tragic, as ever. She got out of the rumpled bed, their bed, and opened the chest of drawers. Moonlight was shining clear through the window. Everything was quiet and still. She took out one of his old jumpers from the drawer and held it to her face. The smell of him was fading. She was losing him, day by day.

The next morning she felt desolate but she knew what she had to do. She must pick up his ashes from the undertaker and put them somewhere. Scatter them. Perhaps in the sea. She thought then of James Turner's ashes, strewn by the monument at Roughtor; the writer who had been in love with Charlotte's ghost. Was she in love with Matt's ghost? She needed the human touch, someone to hold her, physically hold her and love her. Guilt set in then. He had only been gone a matter of months and she was yearning for that feeling of desiring and being desired. It was a betrayal.

The narrow streets and passageways of St Ives were busy with holiday-makers. Poppy made her way towards the lifeboat station, a bulky blue canvas bag slung over one shoulder. She stood in the same spot where she had first seen Matt, playing his guitar. She could sense the electricity in the air, as it had been that day when their eyes had first met.

'Where are you Matt?'

She looked around her, as if to conjure him out of the atmosphere.

'Are you watching me now?'

A seagull with yellow eyes swooped down and landed next to her by the harbour wall. It put its head on one side, looked at her quizzically and strutted on pink webbed feet. She put the canvas bag down carefully. Matt's ashes were inside it. She had been amazed when the undertaker handed her what looked like a bottle-bag one might be given for a birthday celebration. Even his pale, sombre face had not made it seem a serious transaction. She had wanted to burst into irreverent laughter.

'Matt, you would howl. You are reduced to a bottle bag,' she had said to herself, as she signed for the ashes. A small plastic bag had also been given to her, containing Matt's silver Celtic ring. Any secret mirth vanished instantly. How clearly she could see it glinting in the sunshine on his tanned hand as he played his guitar, touching the strings lovingly. And now she was in St Ives, drawn there by some secret force.

The gull had flown off, disturbed by some sudden noise. A feather floated down and landed on the blue bag. Was it a sign from Matt? She remembered reading somewhere that John Lennon had told his son, Julian, that when he died he would send him a white feather, as a sign that he was still watching over him. Years later, an aborigine had presented Julian Lennon with a small white feather. What an amazing story, she had thought at the time. And now her paranormal instincts were roused, down by the sea wall in St Ives.

Matt was here, she felt his presence with an overwhelming feeling of joy. She was sure he had left her a message in the shape of a feather. She felt something amazing could happen at any time. She looked around her, expecting to see something, something different. The sun was strong here by the sea-wall. She could feel its warmth, caressing her bare arms. The canvas bag was at her feet, waiting.

'What are you waiting for, Poppy?'

Matt's voice, whispering in her ear.

'For God's sake, do something with the ashes. You can't just leave them there.'

He was cross with her. She was so indecisive.

She picked up the bag and made her way through narrow streets, known locally as Downalong. Sunlight was flickering over the fishermen's cottages in the maze of cobbled alleys. The town was already coming alive in preparation for the summer season. The smell of fresh paint mingled with the smell of the sea. Years ago it would have been the smell of pilchards and herring. Now the fishing was mainly for mackerel. She had a flashback of eating Cornish mussels with Matt in a restaurant with a view across to Godrevy Lighthouse.

Should she take the steep coastal path towards Zennor? Or walk to The Island, and its chapel? More indecision.

On the cliff path she felt she could breathe more easily. The sea air revitalised her. There was a more determined step as she walked towards The island. The chapel overlooked the white sand of Porthmeor beach, and an iridescent turquoise sea. She could see surfers paddling out on their boards, glistening like seals in black wet-suits. She remembered lying on Porthmeor beach with Rosa next to her, oiled and brown as a gypsy. That seemed so long ago... another lifetime.

'I shall remain pale and interesting,' she had said to Rosa, yet she had been envious of her dark, sultry looks and her beautiful bronzed skin. She remembered how a delicate gold chain gleamed on one of Rosa's pretty brown ankles. Her bright red toenails were sprinkled with silver-white sand. Other memories kicked in.

'I love your marble-white skin,' Matt had whispered, kissing her neck, sending her into a swoon. 'I love your tangled red hair. It's Pre-Raphaelite.'

She had closed her eyes and given herself up to him in the moonlit bedroom of a cottage in the Digey.

But this would not do. She was here to scatter Matt's ashes. She shouldered the bag determinedly and continued along the footpath. The chapel was ahead of her. Its site was dedicated to St Nicholas in the 15th century. This was a good place, she felt. Sea birds swooped and called above her. She clambered down some rocks behind the chapel. She had been told once that this area was a graveyard for ships... and now it would be the place for Matt's remains. For some time she just sat, looking out to sea, letting the sound of the waves wash over her. She imagined the fierce winter gales pounding The Island. A clump of tamarisk near her blew in the sea-breeze. She stood suddenly and unscrewed the top of the container.

'Deep peace of the pure blue sky to you,

Deep peace of the running wave to you.'

She tipped the ashes into the sea below her. Some of them whirled up into the breeze. She watched them dissipate, disappear...

It was done. Matt's ashes were gone.

She was suddenly aware that her eyes were full of stinging tears. Wild, wrenching sobs shook her thin body, and she could not stop them. The sea looked cold and cruel as it washed around the rocks.

She knew it was time to climb up to the cliff path and go home.

THIRTY FIVE

HER voice was low and quiet. 'Annie? It's me. Poppy. I've done it. Matt's ashes.' She paused, 'Give me a ring if you're not working.' She fed Winston, made a fresh cup of coffee and looked out at the moors from her porch. Cattle were grazing nearby in the sunshine. Today in the clarity, the slopes of the tors seemed nearer. A skylark was singing, high in the blue sky. Her washing was pegged out on the line in the patch of garden. It would soon dry in the warmth of the sun.

Poppy's spirits were high. It was a beautiful morning and yesterday she had done what she had been dreading. She leaned against the warm stone drinking her coffee. She felt free, somehow. It was the finality of it all. There was nothing left.

Annie's text said she was working, but she said it was 'bloody brilliant' that Poppy had made herself 'do something' with Matt's remains. Now she could make plans and start to live her life. If only it was that easy, thought Poppy. To start living life to the full again after losing Matt, her great love. To turn her back on her lonely existence in an isolated, but beautiful place. To face up to living in the real world. So, what now?

It was such a wonderful morning and the sunlight and shadows on the moor looked inviting. Poppy took her empty cup inside and searched for her walking boots and an old sweater. Winston watched her from the window-sill, his black coat shining with flashes of blue in the brilliant light.

An hour or so later she was on top of Roughtor,

Cornwall's second highest point, quite breathless after the climb. The sky was cloudless and the view was magnificent all around her, as she stood with heaving chest, swigging from a bottle of spring water. It was a special place, ancient and timeless, where a chapel once stood, surrounded by the mysterious stones. She sat with her back against a huge boulder and she could feel its warmth and power. Perhaps, she mused, that was what her geologist friend meant when he rambled on and on about 'hot rocks'. She closed her eyes and her other senses kicked in. The wind was gentle today, but it still made a strange low whistle around the rocks, in and out of the crevices. She could hear the cries of a bird of prey as it hovered in an arc of blue somewhere nearby. There was a sense of peace here, she felt, in the wild and rugged beauty. Again her eyes closed and she seemed to sleep.

When she next opened her eyes, the tranquillity had been replaced by a festival in full swing, with bands playing, the loud singing of hymns, and banners flying. Below her, at the foot of the tor, were rows of wagons and carts; horses were tethered near the ford and everywhere was bustling humanity. There were literally hundreds and hundreds of people, and most appeared to be listening to a man in sombre black, addressing them from a make-shift wooden platform. A huge banner was in the process of being unravelled by some young men, gradually revealing the words 'Roughtor Teetotal Festival 1843' in massive black letters. Black-bonneted women clustered near the speaker like vultures, their pale faces looking up reverently at his severe, bearded face above a starched collar. His square forefinger was jabbing the air as he drove home some point about the evils of the 'demon drink'.

Poppy watched in absolute amazement. Small boys

in caps and stout boots brushed past her, clambering over rocks like wild goats, elated to escape the confines of the preaching below. They were free to enjoy the breeze on the heights of Roughtor, even if only for a short while, before being dragged back to hear the thundering preacher and his talk of eternal damnation. But the boys were not able to see the woman with tangled red hair sitting there, in her strange, rather manly clothes, for she lived in another time.

'1843 is the year before Charlotte's death,' she breathed. 'All this is going on here at Roughtor, and over on the farm at Penhale Charlotte is still alive, still milking the cows and churning the butter. Or she might even be here, in the midst of all this madness.'

But even as she said it she knew that she would not find Charlotte here, not caught up in the Temperance movement. And what about Matthew Weeks, who must also still be alive? Would Matthew be here midst the crowd? She felt not, somehow. He was probably walking out on the moor somewhere, enjoying the free time away from the drudgery of the farm. Was Charlotte with him somewhere? Were they laughing together at some little thing, unaware of the darkness looming in the year ahead of them, when both of them would face violent, tragic deaths?

A shiver ran through her. It was becoming damp now on the tor. The loud hymn-singing reached a crescendo and petered out. A band struck up and the milling crowd appeared to search out refreshments from the many booths scattered around. On the outskirts of the gathering were a couple of stalls set up by publicans where men were flagrantly swigging cider and other intoxicating drinks rather than the permitted tea of the Temperance tables. There was also a wrestling ring in a far corner, next to a row of harnessed donkeys, which hinted at racing to come. So, she mused, the local opposition to the Temperance movement was out in strength..

Time seemed to move quickly on, until the light faded a little and many of the wagons and carts, jammed with women and younger children, were moving in a straggling line away from the gathering. Some men were on horseback and at least one lumbering wagon became stuck in mud near the ford. Older children walked or jogged alongside the farm-carts. Booths were being taken down and packed away. The wooden staging, where the speakers had stood, was now a mere skeleton.

Yet in one corner of the festival, dancing and drunken singing continued. The teetotallers had failed to stop the sale of intoxicating drink and the ensuing revelry. Two inebriated men, who had their jackets off and sleeves rolled up, were throwing punches at each other. Wild-looking women drunkenly clutched mugs of beer, others showed a mass of unwashed petticoats as they cavorted and danced. It was an escape for them from the grind of their everyday lives, if only for an hour or two.

Poppy watched the scene, with all its colour and warmth and vitality, then suddenly realised she was not the only watcher. There in the darkening evening she recognised the face of Isaac Cory, a lascivious expression on his face. Once again, he seemed to be playing the role of 'the watcher', his narrowed eyes never once leaving the frolics of the women, as they flirted and sang with the men, now lost in drink.

The revelry faded quickly before her... and then brightened once more. It was the same place, but the jostling crowd was much, much bigger than before. Banners flew, bands played, but something was different. A huge banner proclaimed proudly 'Roughtor Teetotal Festival 1844'. Time had played its tricks once more.

''Twas just there they found Charlotte Dymond's body,' said a woman next to her, pointing out a place to her huge-bosomed companion, who was craning her neck and tucking into a saffron bun at the same time.

'See? Where the black flag is?'

True enough a black flag had been fixed down in the marshy ground.

''Twas on that very spot they found the poor maid. Horrible sight 'twere, by all accounts.'

She paused for effect.

'Blood everywhere, Mrs Pethick said. And to think that such a thing could happen on a Sunday too. Only two months since.'

The saffron-bun eater hurriedly bolted her remaining morsel and brushed the crumbs off a black bodice which strained over her chest.

'Let's walk down and have a closer look,' she said, excitedly. Like two brood mares breaking into a lumbering canter, the women descended the slope towards the stream.

Poppy followed them slowly and at a distance, thinking of the murder that had taken place there. She sat for a while on an outcrop of granite, with her eyes closed, listening to the sighing of the wind. When she opened them again, the site of the Temperance rally was deserted once more. Below her by the stream stood not a black flag on a stick but a solid granite memorial, now partially covered with lichen and moss. She read the words, carved so many years ago.

'Monument erected by public subscription in memory of Charlotte Dymond who was murdered by Matthew Weeks, Sunday, April 14th, 1844.'

For nearly a hundred and seventy years, Charlotte and Matthew's names had been carved in granite, together, below the frowning face of Roughtor.

THIRTY SIX

A TAXI was parked outside Poppy's cottage when she eventually returned from her rambles at Roughtor. The driver was standing with his back against the car, smoking a cigarette moodily and looking meaningfully at his watch. The passenger seat was empty. Then a woman with shiny honey-blonde hair teetered round the corner of the cottage on a pair of ridiculously high shoes. Poppy's heart sank.

Her mother had appeared out of nowhere, no warning, no phone call. Oh my God, she thought, how would she cope? She tried but failed to adopt a surprised, welcoming smile. The taxi soon roared off up the lane, its driver looking extremely pleased with an inflated fare. Poppy's mother picked her way through nuggets of sheep droppings and was soon inside the cottage, taking it all in; and by her sucked-in expression she was not over-impressed with what she saw.

'Honey, what the hell are you thinking of, living out here on your own?'

Angie, or Angel as she now insisted on being called, was frowning at her only daughter in disbelief.

'How can you live in a terrible place like this? In the middle of nowhere, in this absolute dump? It's like something out of Dickens.'

She shook her head and looked around her, searching for something to redeem it. But there was nothing positive for Angel to comment on, so she changed tack.

'Come on, give me a hug.'

Poppy kissed her mother's cold cheek and had a quick whiff of expensive perfume. She pulled back.

'What on earth are you doing over here in England? Or in Cornwall, should I say?'

'Brad has business over here, in London. He thought I'd like it if we spent a couple of days down in the west-country, so I could see you and catch up.'

'So where are you staying?'

Poppy looked around for Angel's suitcase and quickly realised, with relief, that her mother had no intentions of slumming it in an old cottage on Bodmin Moor.

'We're at the Headland Hotel in Newquay for a couple of days. Brad's playing golf at St Enodoc with some business friend, so I thought I'd pop up the road to see you, darling.'

Angel paused for breath, and took a long hard look at her daughter.

'You look absolutely terrible, honey. Too thin by half, no boobs, and those dreadful, shapeless clothes. As for your hair... well, it needs conditioning and cutting.'

'Don't start to criticise already, Mum. Yes I'm thin, but I'm eating like a horse if you must know. And my clothes are just old jeans and a sweater, just like you used to wear.'

She took a deep breath,.

'What else should I wear for walking out on the moors? Your designer outfit? Stiletto shoes and a Gucci handbag perhaps?'

'Sorry darling.'

Angel reached into the very handbag, with beautifully manicured nails, and brought out some exotic-looking American cigarettes and a gold lighter. She perched on the edge of the saggy sofa, looking for all the world like an expensive piece of brittle bone-china.

Winston hissed at Angel malevolently from behind the log basket and slunk towards his retreat under the staircase.

Poppy could not help but smile secretly. She made them both a coffee and took a roll-up from its battered tin, while her mother regaled her with lengthy stories of her opulent lifestyle in the States.

'So you're happy then?' Poppy asked.

Angel shot her a withering look.

'What do you think?'

'Well you weren't happy with Dad, so I'm glad you've got it right this time.'

Poppy put her dog-end in the ash-tray and picked up the mugs. She put them in the cluttered sink, pausing to look out the window at the lurid light over the moors. Her mother walked over to the window and said in an unbelievably gentle voice: 'I'm really sorry about Matt, sweetheart. I couldn't believe it when I heard from my friends at Bude. You really should have told me yourself, darling.'

Poppy nodded. She could not trust herself to answer this new softly-spoken mother, remembering only the tears and screaming and selfishness that her darling father had had to cope with for years.

'Did Matt jump? Or did he fall off the cliffs?'

The bluntness made her start. This was more like her real mother.

'The inquest said it was suicide. But I'm really not sure.'

Her voice was weary, she was so tired with thinking of it all.

'He fell off the sheer cliffs at Morwenstow when he was out of his mind. I like to think it was a tragic accident, but sometimes I really wonder.'

'But why the hell are you living out here Poppy?

You need friends around you, lively company to cheer you up. Not hide away in an isolated place like this, with just a mangy cat for company.'

Angel frowned.

'Have you still got that farmer-friend, Jack, or whatever he was called? The one with the friendly face who was always mad about you?'

'Yup. And his name is Josh. Actually he's been brilliant, right from the day that he found out about Matt. He drove straight up to see me at Morwenstow, and he's given me bags of support ever since.'

She turned to face her mother and noticed, as if for the first time, her incredibly white, even teeth and her new polished look in her carefully chosen clothes.

'And is this Josh a wealthy young farmer?'

Angel blew smoke up into the air.

'Wondered when we would come to that.'

Poppy's voice was dangerously low. Then, in a louder voice, she said: 'Apparently no farmers are wealthy these days, or so they say. That's why they've had to diversify, you know, barn renovations and farm holidays for city kids. Stuff like that.'

'Sounds interesting, well the bit about the barns does. You always used to say you'd love to live in a converted barn, darling.'

'Please don't start match-making the minute you see me. I'm more than capable of sorting out my own life.'

Even as she said it, Poppy had a sudden flashback of Steve's cocky grin on that wet day in Bodmin before he'd attempted to rape her. For that was what it had been... she realised that only too clearly now.

'Will I meet this Jack, or Josh, or whatever he's called?'

Angel stretched out her left hand, admiring the enormous diamond that winked and sparkled on her wedding finger as she turned it in the light.

'I doubt it very much,' Poppy responded dryly. She hoped fervently that Josh would not suddenly turn up unannounced. It would be purgatory, as her grandmother used to say. If only that bloody taxi would come back and whisk this new glossy mother away. Take her back to Newquay. To America. Anywhere, so she would not disturb her own quiet existence on the moor.

It was to be another three hours before Angel made her tottering exit from Penhale Cottage. Copious amounts of brandy had been consumed, by both mother and daughter before the taxi pulled up. It was the same driver, now buoyant at the thought of another 'fare-killing'. He smiled as he helped a sozzled Angel into the taxi, its engine still running.

'Not looking quite so polished now, Mother,' Poppy smiled to herself as she stood at the porch, waving. The taxi drove off up the lane in the moonlight. She turned back into her home and spoke to the cat now emerging from the shadows.

'Thank God she's gone.'

She bent to stroke Winston's soft fur. The ash-tray was overflowing with crushed cigarette ends with distinctive gold bands. There was a faint smell of expensive perfume in the air.

'Winston,' she sighed, 'I don't even know who the hell she is any more.'

THIRTY SEVEN

THE town of Bodmin was crammed with people in
the bright sunshine. A sombre procession was
wending its way down Fore Street, clad in the plain attire
of monks, led by a Crucifer and a couple of servers,
followed by priests wearing cassocks and lace-edged
surplices. Between them they were carrying something,
a holy relic perhaps, held reverently on a small bier. A
murmur arose from the restless crowd, lining the street.

''Tis St. Petroc's bones,' said a pious-looking
woman, crossing herself as they processed past her in the
direction of the ancient parish church. 'God bless him.'

Colourful stalls had been erected on the roadside
since early morning and soon they were doing brisk
business, now that the serious part of the day's business
had been done. A hog was roasting on the corner of
Honey Street, its loud sizzling and appetising smell
wafting through the mass of people beginning to
accumulate on the Folly, outside the Assize Courts.

'What be they all waiting for?' the querulous voice
of a visitor to Bodmin town asked.

'For the trial, you numbskull.'

Loud laughter filled the air, heavy with blue smoke
from the hog-roast.

'Whose trial be 'e talking of?'

The visitor was not to be put off, obviously.

'Don't 'e knaw nothing? 'Tis the trial of the Mayor
of Bodmin heeself.'

More laughter.

'Not that 'e stands a chance, mind. We d'all knaw

Mayor Boyer'll end up on the gallows. Why else d'ye reckon all we be 'ere today? 'Tis a sight not to be missed by man nor beast.'

There was a vehement nodding of heads, young and old. Poppy and Annie pushed their way through the crowds at the Folly, wondering at the chaos. Ahead of them was a makeshift gallows. Two local men were struggling with their 'authentic' rustic costumes in the crush, as they stood at the bottom of wooden steps. Children gazed up in awe at a dangling rope as they licked toffee-apples and ice-creams.

'How macabre is that?'

Annie shook her head in disbelief.

'To celebrate a hanging that happened back in the 15th century?'

Poppy took a swig from her bottle of spring-water. She could feel the sweat gathering on her forehead and in her armpits.

'It was your idea to come here today. To help me with my research, you said.'

She looked at the mass of people, clustering around Mount Folly with an air of excited anticipation.

'Well I think we probably picked the wrong day, Annie.'

'The Mayor of Bodmin was instructed to erect a gibbet outside his residence by Sir Anthony Kingston, the Provost-Marshal of King Edward IV's army. It was to execute some rebels, or so he was told.'

Annie stopped reading her pamphlet aloud, having been pushed to one side by an enormous woman in sumptuous medieval costume.

'Hey, what's your problem?' she shouted. The woman swept past like a ship in full sail, oblivious to all but her purpose.

Annie found her place in the pamphlet and read

loudly: 'It appears Mayor Boyer was thought to be guilty of insurrection. When he had finished wining and dining the King's officers, the Mayor was led out by the Provost-Marshal, protesting, and he was put on his own gallows to hang in front of the good people of Bodmin. Hoist by his own petard, you could say.'

Poppy did not seem to be listening. Her head was whirling with all the noise and excitement of Heritage Day, with the clamouring of the crowd, as the bewildered but elaborately-costumed Mayor was dragged out by the King's officers. Loud cheers erupted from the packed crowd.

'Hang him!' shouted someone close by, and soon the chant was taken up by those surrounding the gibbet.

'Hang him! Hang him!'

The voices rang out, while the two men sweated in their costumes as they pushed the loudly-protesting Mayor up the steps. A black-hooded executioner held the noose ready for the prisoner's neck. The man faced 'the good people of Bodmin' who were by now baying for his blood. He pulled himself together, smoothing down his somewhat dishevelled attire, to make his final dramatic speech to the world in which he would, of course, plead his innocence… The man looked thin and wretched from the back. It seemed that he was on the verge of collapse, Poppy thought, in a state of near panic herself.

'He've had Communion in the prison church service, don't 'e know,' a woman whispered loudly to her companion. 'I could hear the tolling of the chapel bell where I d'live, up at Town End. They say 'e've been in a terrible state since 'e were sentenced. But 'e wrote out 'is confession good n'proper.'

'Be 'e completely mazed? 'E couldn't read nor write a word himself. So who wrote 'is so-called confession, I say?'

The woman shook her head at the injustice of it all.

Poppy's heart lurched. This was no re-enactment. Even as she watched, feeling sick to her stomach, the man turned his head and she saw clearly the traumatised face of Matthew Weeks approaching the drop. He clutched a handkerchief in his hand, but his arms were tied and his movements seemed to be faltering. The chapel bell was tolling its melancholy summons, not to Communion now, but to call the immense crowd to the execution.

'Shame 'tis that the train on the Wadebridge-Bodmin railway idn't running today,' an elderly man moaned. 'Us had to walk the seven miles as 'tis engine-cleaning day.'

''Twas running for the 'anging of they Lightfoot brothers four year ago. Niver seen the train so packed in me life,' said his stocky friend, wiping a sweating brow with a handkerchief.

'Still, Bodmin is full to the brim. Nawthing like an execution day for good business.'

The first man nodded with satisfaction.

'I 'ad a yarn with an old biddy who walked all the way from Liskeard. 'Er was fair near collapsin', but a few swigs from a gin bottle outside the Railway Inn soon revived 'er flagging spirits.'

His face lit up at the memory.

'I bought a copy of the prisoner's last dyin' speech, down Pool Street,' said a red-faced woman, flapping a dubious printed sheet above their heads.

'You must be pretty mazed then, fer 'e 'adn't made 'is last speech yet.'

Much laughter was the response from the jostling crowd.

'Look! Tis the executioner!'

'What? That ancient-lookin' man with the grey hair? Can't be.'

The hangman, George Mitchell, looked about seventy. He had travelled all the way from Somerset to mete out capital punishment on Matthew Weeks.

''Tidn't like the old days. Then us 'ad lots of good hangings to watch,' came a hoarse voice.

Poppy took an intake of breath, as she saw the hangman adjust the rope around Matthew's neck. Poor, poor Matthew. It seemed to her that he could hardly stand. The cap was pulled down over his face, which was blanched with fear of his approaching death.

'Last dying speech!'

Many in the crowd of some twenty thousand shouted at the scaffold, hoping for even more drama to spice up their day.

'Speech! Speech!'

But they were to be disappointed, for poor Matthew said not one word. He seemed to faint away as the Chaplain, Reverend Kendall, read a final prayer, asking God for his mercy on the condemned man.

'You must listen. He didn't do it,' Poppy found herself shrieking at the top of her voice. 'He didn't murder Charlotte Dymond.'

But no one took any notice of a solitary voice, lost amongst the hubbub of such an immense gathering.

The gaol's chaplain and the executioner withdrew solemnly from the platform. A deadly silence fell over those watching. The bolts grated as they were withdrawn and the trap-door fell with the most terrible sound. Matthew's body fell and hung lifeless on the rope, swinging before them.

His handkerchief was still grasped in his hand, even in death. The glass buttons on his jacket winked in the sunlight as his body turned on the creaking rope. Some of the many women in the crowd appeared to faint. Others screamed and shrieked loudly.

Children cried and were gathered up into arms. There was much pushing and jostling in front of the gaol and up on the hillside.

'The body'll be dangling there fer an hour an' a minute,' said an old man's voice, with the greatest of satisfaction.

'Well you be the expert,' was his friend's admiring reply. 'Niver knaw'd a man to've seen so many hexecutions as you, Jack.'

Poppy turned away, feeling an overwhelming nausea sweeping over her.

The crowd was beginning to disperse now, many making their way into the streets with their laden stalls, some with 'confessions' for sale. The twenty-two taverns in the borough of Bodmin were soon overflowing with drunks.

Matthew's body was taken down, after an hour and a minute, as Jack had quite rightly said, ready for burial in the precincts of the gaol, in the plot reserved for those executed.

A reporter from a local newspaper scribbled: 'There was much water in the grave which had been prepared for the body of Matthew Weeks. I noticed that his coffin floated, as his remains were laid to rest.'

Poppy looked desperately for Annie. She found herself back on the Folly. A street theatre company was entertaining the crowd surrounding the Shire Hall. Somewhere a brass band was playing loudly and smiling children were dancing down the streets. The re-enactment of the hanging of Mayor Boyer had evidently ended and the gibbet had been cleared away.

'Hi! I couldn't stand that morbid bit so I've been looking at the craft stalls.'

Annie held out an unusual piece of hand-painted pottery.

'Thought you might like it for your lovely cottage.'

Poppy was as white as a sheet as she took the present and quietly murmured her thanks.

'Are you OK? You look as if you've seen another ghost!'

'I think I have.'

Poppy forced a smile.

'I've just witnessed a hanging. Not the re-enactment with men in silly costumes, Annie.'

She searched for her tin of roll-ups and lit one with shaking hands. She inhaled deeply.

'I have just been an onlooker at the hanging of Matthew Weeks, right here in Bodmin, back in the year 1844.'

Thirty Eight

ANNIE had been talking to her in a kind, understanding voice for some minutes, like someone might talk to a child. Poppy just nodded in response when she felt it was expected of her. They were sitting in Annie's car. It was jammed in between a shining scarlet Audi and an old rust bucket in one of Bodmin's packed car parks. The town was still heaving from the sheer volume of people enjoying Bodmin Riding. The procession of decorated horses and costumed children was making its way slowly through the streets, lined with proud parents clicking cameras. A couple of drunken youths lounged in Priory Park by the duck pond, swigging out of beer-cans. There was a pause when Poppy blew her nose and wiped a smudge of black mascara from her cheek.

'I'm fine now. It was a shock, that's all.'

'I'm not surprised. But was it a worse shock than seeing your bloody mother turn up out of the blue?'

Annie handed her another tissue. She motioned towards Poppy's nose. Poppy managed a small smile and soon they were laughing out loud at stories of Angel, her terrible mother, teetering between the nubs of sheep-shit on expensive high-heels.

'You really do believe that thing about Matthew not being the real murderer, don't you?'

Annie fiddled with her long fair hair, twisting it into a thick rope.

'Have you had a good look at the news reports from his trial?'

'Some of them. The whole thing stinks. Matthew's defence only lasted a bare hour. And guess who his solicitor was? A man called Richard Peter from a legal practice in Launceston. Think Annie, who did poor Charlotte work for?'

She paused a moment.

'Mrs. Peter, of Davidstow parish. Matthew Weeks' defence was actually prepared by some sort of relative of her dead husband.'

'Hmm,' murmured Annie thoughtfully. 'Don't think they would allow it for one moment today.'

'And Charlotte's death certificate even said the cause of her death was wilful murder by Matthew Weeks. And that was over three months before his trial. Talk about guilty before proven innocent.

'It seems Richard Peter then passed the case on to some barrister called Slade. He turned out to be Matthew's only representative in the courtroom. The prosecution had a Queen's Counsel, as well as two others. The set-up makes you wonder what was really going on.'

There was a brief silence in the car.

'And another thing, nearly all the evidence was circumstantial, like Matthew's boots were muddy when he came back to Penhale Farm that fateful Sunday evening, which the Prosecution thought proved he'd murdered a girl on the moor. Well his boots would have been muddy anyway. He admitted he'd gone for a walk with Charlotte that day. But it does not bloody well prove that he killed her.'

A long silence ensued as they both brooded on her words.

'Come on, let's try and get out of here. The procession seems to have passed and it's getting quieter.'

Annie started up the car. The youths watched

lethargically as she manoeuvred out of the tight spot, and then they returned to their drinking, slumped on the low wall surrounding the duck pond.

Half an hour later they were up on the open moor. In the distance were the tors, bathed in late afternoon sunlight. A small cloud drifted overhead, causing shadows to pass over the expanse of grassland. Annie pulled in by the roadside and flung open her door.

'Smell that. Isn't it heavenly? Just the fresh moorland wind blowing, the smell of dry grass and heather, with a tang of the marshes in the air. Do you fancy a walk for a bit? It might help clear your head.'

Poppy looked at her bright red leather sandals ruefully.

'If you really want. But not a long hike.'

She stuck her foot out by way of explanation. They talked as they tramped through the ferns for an hour or so, enjoying the warmth of the sun on their bare arms. Sweaters were tied casually round their waists and their faces seemed to glow in the mellow light. Annie dug into her pocket and pulled out a squashed piece of a chocolate bar, which looked absolutely awful but was in fact delicious. The freedom of the moors infected them.

'I've been thinking.'

Poppy stopped and knelt to fish out bits of grass and fern caught in her sandals.

'I really think I need to go to Charlotte's stone at Roughtor.'

She stood up, a distant look on her face.

'Perhaps just to sit there for a while and meditate.'

'What, now?'

Annie looked unhappy at the thought.

'No not now,' was Poppy's muffled reply, as she bent once more to pull a prickle out of her big toe.

'Thank God for that. I've had enough for one day.'

The sun was sinking slowly in the west. Annie looked at her watch.

'In fact I think I should drop you off at the cottage pretty soon. I must get back to Lanson before too long.'

She sighed.

'My brother's calling in with his new girlfriend this evening.'

Poppy remembered Annie's younger brother, Jake, as tall, dark and extremely good-looking. He changed his girlfriends as frequently as his socks. But he always fell madly in love with each one and was unhealthily possessive about them.

'For some inexplicable reason, he parades all his girlfriends in front of me for my approval,' said Annie, shaling her head despairingly. 'Not that he takes any notice if I later make a comment about the unsuitability of his latest lover. He just likes a challenge, that's all. It's a case of "if I'm not going to have her, no one else will". Crazy really. I mean he's so damn good-looking with those amazing dark eyes that most young girls fall at his feet anyway.'

As Poppy listened to Annie's talk of Jake, another good-looking face came to her. Dark eyes danced before her... the eyes of Thomas Prout, as he talked and flirted with Charlotte Dymond in the yard of Penhale Farm, and out on the moor, and in the country lanes.

Why had Tommy come to the farm that fateful Sunday morning to see Charlotte? He had sat by the fire on the settle in the farmhouse kitchen. Then when he got up to leave, Charlotte had grabbed her bonnet and followed him outside. Was Tommy determined to woo pretty Charlotte away from Matthew? Was it 'a challenge' to the man who liked to goad Matthew Weeks whenever possible? Poppy remembered seeing the light in Charlotte's eyes as she had looked down at Tommy

Prout's handsome face in the muddy lane. They had arranged to meet at Tremail Chapel on the very evening of Charlotte's disappearance. Tommy had said so at the inquest. He went to the chapel, or so he'd said, but she was not there. Of course she was not there, Charlotte was lying out on the moor with her throat cut. Her lovely careless youth had been cruelly taken from her. But if it was not by Matthew Weeks, then who had been responsible? More and more, Poppy's suspicions were hardening in another direction completely.

Her mind was somewhere else, in another time, when they returned to Annie's car.

Across the moor in the sinking sunlight was the grim, silent outline of Roughtor, with Brown Willy at its side.

'If only stones could talk,' Poppy murmured yet again, as she looked across at the tors. The sun was reflected in the metallic body of Annie's car as they climbed in, ready to make the short journey home.

Thirty Nine

POPPY knew she was feeling better when she woke up because she desperately needed to paint. It seemed ages since she'd felt this urgency. The need to get out of bed and throw on her old smock and rifle through her brushes and paints. There was a clutter of canvasses and sketchbooks, crayons and boxes of chalks, all neglected in the spidery corner under the stairs.

There was nothing quite like the feeling of opening fat new tubes of paint and squeezing the bright virgin paint on to a palette. It was probably better than sex, she thought at that very moment. Well, perhaps not. But that was another thing. It seemed ages since she last had good sex. Matt had been dead for months and months, but it felt like years. Her body had been dead too, she realised now. Dried up. Skeletal.

She'd had a real shock when she'd looked at herself, naked, in the bedroom mirror. Dragging on shapeless baggy jeans, she and had to pull in the belt so far it needed a new hole. She pulled her tangled hair up and twisted it into a loose knot, pinned carelessly on top of her head with a silver Celtic hair clasp she'd bought in the Highlands.

The blank canvas had been quietly and patiently waiting for her under the stairs all the time. She blew the dust off and rooted through brushes, some old and paint-covered, some brand-new and begging to be used. She pulled out her easel and set it up, then dragged it over to the doorway rucking the mats. The morning light filtered through the open door. It felt good to be working again.

She worked solidly for several hours, sketching lightly and furiously in pencil first, then adding luxurious paint, sometimes with a palette knife, enjoying the feel of the textures she was creating. Winston sat upright, watching as still as a mummified cat or an Egyptian statue. His hidey-hole under the stairs had been ransacked and now he needed to see what the fuss was about. Poppy kept the kettle on the boil, drinking mug after mug of black coffee, quickly eating snatches of rice cakes or chunks of cheese.

It was a semi-abstract of the moor with its stones and heather. She could breathe it, taste it, through the open door. It was in her head and now it was appearing on canvas in purples and green tones, with shadows of greys. She tried to avoid too much black, but there were reflections of light from a brooding sky on a pool of flat water.

It was late afternoon when she laid down her brushes for the day, wiped her fingers on an old rag and stood back from her easel, head critically on one side. The sound of an engine on the lane, hidden behind the few stunted trees, made her look up from her work. It was Josh's jeep. He climbed out of the dusty vehicle with a huge smile on his face, sun-bleached hair tousled like a hay-stack. She suddenly realised how she had missed seeing him. It was days. Nearly a week, she thought.

'I see you've been doing some painting. Bloody fantastic.'

He swept her into his arms and gave her a hug. She could feel the hardness of his muscles as his strong arms enfolded her. He kissed the top of her head and then brushed her cheek with his mouth.

'Look out! I'm covered in paint,' she laughed up at him. He saw that her eyes were laughing too, no longer looking at him like green chips of ice.

There was a smudge of purple paint on her forehead, like a bruise.

'What the hell!'

He looked at her and became suddenly serious. He bent his head and kissed her tentatively on her mouth. This time she did not pull back like someone stung. It was Josh who broke away first.

'Sorry,' he said quietly, in his deep voice. Poppy felt her heart thumping madly.

'It's OK.'

In fact it was surprisingly more than OK, she thought, picking up a couple of brushes, sticky with paint, and going over to the sink to wash them out. She was glad her back was to him. He stood in the open doorway, quietly contemplating the dwindling sunlight over the tops of the tors, dwelling on the unexpected kiss they had just shared.

'Do you fancy a drive to the coast or somewhere?'

Josh looked at her back in its paint-covered smock, her hair tumbling down in disarray.

'Not the sea, not this time. But I'd really like to walk over to Roughtor ford.'

She turned to look at him standing in the doorway. A halo of light illuminated his hair, so she could not really gauge the expression on his face.

'Fine, if that's what you want.'

'I'll clear this mess away and have a quick wash.'

She flashed him a brilliant smile.

'Can you just drag my easel away from the door?'

They walked away from the cottage and up the lane. Soon they were near Trevilian Gate, then onto the open moor and striking out towards the outline of Roughtor. At first there was a tangible tension, as neither mentioned what had just happened between them. And something had happened, they both knew.

'What's the latest on your murder story? I presume this is why we are walking out here.'

Josh looked at her striding out purposefully beside him in her walking boots.

'Not a lot different, but I know for sure that Matthew Weeks did not kill Charlotte Dymond.'

Poppy looked determined, set on reaching the granite monument where the crime had actually taken place.

'Whoever did kill Charlotte must have committed the deed after about seven in the evening. He must have murdered her and then buried some of her bits and pieces, like her bonnet and shawl and stuff. Then he must have disappeared into thin air.'

She stopped walking.

'If it was Matthew... and it wasn't... he'd have had to limp back to Penhale farm across miles of moorland in the darkness and fog and then seem his usual calm self. Anyway he would have been covered in blood if he'd killed her.'

Josh nodded in agreement at this. Many times he'd seen pigs having their throats slit and he'd hated the shrill squealing and the sudden gush of the blood. They tramped on in silence for a bit, then it was Josh's turn to stop.

'So why did he confess if he did not actually commit the murder?'

Poppy stopped too.

'It's obvious. He was exhausted after weeks of questions and suspicions, he was frightened to death. No one believed anything he said. They were all against him back at the farm, thinking he was hiding something. In the end, he must have felt guilty and depressed.'

A flock of birds flew overhead, their wings making a rustling sound in flight.

'Matthew needed to talk to someone in the gaol. Who was there to talk to? Only the chaplain.'

She looked up as the birds circled and flew over them once more.

'The authorities wanted a confession to justify the sentence they would give him, which the majority of people expected anyway. We know Matthew was illiterate, so he could not write his own confession. So it had to be taken down in notes and bits of reports and moulded into some sort of a confession. Then he would put his mark to it, even though he could not read it through to see what was written.'

'Poor bugger,' said Josh.

'In his desperate state in the gaol, Matthew must have trusted the chaplain completely,' added Poppy.

They walked on silently for a while, picking their way through marshy tufts of grass, both thinking of tragic Matthew Weeks, convicted on circumstantial evidence that would be rubbished and thrown out of any present-day court.

The terrain was rougher now, the ground becoming boggy as they descended towards the stream, the stony face of Roughtor ever the backdrop. A few moorland ponies splashed through the stream. Their hooves stumbled as they came up from the stream on to the bank, making their way to a stony track. The wind blew across the marsh grasses and the bubbling call of a curlew made them both shiver. Before them, on the bank of the stream, stood the tall, granite pillar. Charlotte's monument, brooding over the slate-grey water course where she had met her death.

FORTY

THEY stood side by side and looked at the memorial stone. Lichen clung to the granite, testament to the time it had stood here above the green tufts of marsh.

'In memory of Charlotte Dymond,' Josh read aloud, 'who was murdered here by Matthew Weeks on Sunday April 14, 1844.'

Poppy sat down wearily on the rough granite that formed the base of the pillar. She looked up at him.

'You see? It is written in stone, for the entire world to see, to confirm his guilt.'

They both listened to the sound of water trickling between the stones in the stream. Again the mournful, liquid call of the curlew came across the marshes.

'It makes you think though,' said Josh. 'Just who actually organised putting a monument here back in 1844? And who went round collecting the subscriptions from the public? It must have cost a bit back then.'

The light was fading and Josh pulled her to her feet. She was shivering.

'We need to get back to the cottage before it gets dark.'

She nodded and took one last look around at the lonely place. She had expected to 'see' something, feel something in this haunted place. But there was no sign of Charlotte's presence. She would return on her own, she thought.

It was comforting to be back at the cottage. Josh made up the fire and lit it, while Poppy pulled the curtains across. They drank mugs of coffee, liberally laced with brandy. Winston slunk over to the hearth and turned his gleaming back to them, before washing himself fastidiously in front of the flames.

'We ran out of time there this evening,' Poppy mused aloud, cupping her hands around her warm mug. She sloshed some more brandy into it and proffered the bottle to Josh. He shook his head and stood up suddenly, announcing his intention to go home and get an early night. There were bullocks to load at the crack of dawn the next morning, for Hallworthy market. She tried not to look too disappointed, remembering the sudden and unexpected kiss they had shared before their walk. She was surprised at her strengthening feeling that what she would have really liked was for him to stay with her longer. He did not linger. There was no follow-up kiss by the doorway. He disappeared into his jeep, the headlights reflecting in the eyes of some cattle and sheep sheltering near the walls which formed the boundary between the cottage and the moor.

It was still not late. She tried to read, but could not settle. She peeped out of the corner of the curtains but the scene was one of nature in perfect stillness. No face at the window. No ghosts at Roughtor ford. Who could help her in her search for the truth? To bridge the gap between life and death?

And then it came to her. Gweniver. Gweniver could help. She was a mystic, a medium even. Poppy took a huge gulp of brandy. She would ring her in the morning. Perhaps Gweniver would even feel up to a trip to Roughtor, where she spent some of her own childhood.

Sixteen hours later Poppy's car made its way up the road out of Camelford and turned right at the sign towards Roughtor. In the front passenger seat, barely able to see much over the dashboard, was Gweniver, her brown, inquisitive monkey eyes taking everything in: the recently-built bungalows, the spring flowers in carefully tended gardens with evidence of new growth, the few people walking dogs along the narrow lane.

'Haven't been out this way for years,' she sighed nostalgically to Poppy, who was driving uncharacteristically slowly. ''Tis all different from how I d' remember it.'

The car approached the parking area for Roughtor. Poppy parked near to the track that led down to the stream. She began to think how impulsive she had been to bring Gweniver, when the dear old thing could not even walk very far. Josh would probably be furious with her. Still, it was too late now, they were there. Fait accompli.

Gweniver climbed painfully out of the car, but her eyes sparkled as she looked around. The rugged beauty of the moor inspired her and she immediately felt in tune with the place. A gleam of sunlight lit the stream below, turning it momentarily to liquid gold. A kestrel hovered in the sky above them.

'Come on then, maid. I'm not a cripple you know, I can still manage to walk down to the ford.'

Gweniver leaned heavily on her ebony walking stick and tottered a few steps over the rough surface of the car park. Poppy groaned inwardly, guilt kicking in, when she realised just how frail this tiny woman was, with her back cruelly bent over.

Somehow they managed to reach the ford and Gweniver sat hunched on an outcrop of rock, her shrewd eyes looking around her. On the bank to their right was Charlotte's memorial stone, surrounded by marsh and tangled barbed wire. It was obvious that Josh's grandmother would never be able to get through either the wire or the boggy ground.

Gweniver perched on her stone and closed her eyes,

absorbing the wild landscape with all her senses. Wisps of silvery-white hair blew around her wrinkled brown face. Her claw-like hand clutched the carved wooden stick tightly. There was something hawk-like in her appearance, perched on a rock before taking off into flight. Her purple pashmina flapped in the pure, cold air. The only sounds were that of the wind and the trickling of clear moorland water over the stones. Above them, the grey face of Roughtor brooded majestically on its secrets.

Poppy sat by the side of the stream, listening to its music. She too closed her eyes to sharpen her perception. When she opened them again she had lost all sense of time. She turned to look at Gweniver and saw that her rocky perch was empty. Panicking, she clambered to her feet and scanned the surrounding area. She was suddenly aware of movement near the memorial stone. Gweniver stood at its base, holding a pendulum. It was whirling violently. Poppy suddenly turned icy-cold. She watched the strange old woman, muttering quietly in the shadow of the stone. How had she got there? And who was she talking to? Poppy shivered. She felt absolutely freezing. Had Gweniver made contact with a spirit? If so, was it the spirit of Charlotte Dymond?

How long she stood there watching, she could not say. She was aware that something seemed to brush past her, an invisible something. Whoever it was, she felt as if she was in a nightmare. She knew she could not look behind her in this place of loneliness, it was as if something or someone resented her being there.

In a trembling voice she started to recite the Lord's Prayer aloud in Cornish: 'Agan Tas-ny, us yn nef, Benygys re bo dha Hanow...'

FORTY ONE

THE nervous bullocks had been unloaded at Hallworthy, hooves slipping and stumbling down the tailgate of the cattle lorry. Josh had helped load them in the half-light at their farm at St Clether. He had risen early after a sleepless night, having lain awake into the small hours, tossing and turning in his bed, always coming back to that impromptu kiss with Poppy. The coldness that had invaded her soul after Matt's death was melting. Things had changed, he knew. But for all that he was wary.

Now the market was noisy and in full swing: auctioneers gabbling, farmers leaning over the rails of the pens having a yarn, loud talk of 'good conformation' as the livestock was surveyed, or general gossip between friends about how the missus was and the next social event at chapel.

Josh turned away to answer his mobile. He put his fingers to his other ear. His father's voice was barely audible, asking him to pick up a spare part from Camelford. He was glad to leave the racket of the market behind him and just drive. He listened to music as he drove, passing through Davidstow in the wake of a milk tanker making its way to the cheese factory on the edge of the old aerodrome.

It took some time to get the required part in Camelford. He sat in his jeep and rolled a cigarette slowly and did not feel like going straight home, even though his father would be in a mood with him later. He licked the cigarette paper and reached a decision. He wasn't far from Boscastle, he'd visit his gran. She was always glad to see him and she might have even made some of her famous pasties.

Josh was surprised when his gran did not answer his 'special' knock at the door of her white-washed cottage. He stepped back, finding it locked but he knew she kept a key round the back under a plant-pot. The old tabby cat watched him suspiciously as he found the key, unlocked the back door and bent his head under the low doorway into the kitchen. No appetising smell of pasties, not a sign of the usual baking on the wooden scrubbed table. Crystals hanging in the window tinkled in the breeze from the open door. The cat had followed him inside and was crunching some nibbles in a dish by the door. He opened one of his gran's biscuit tins and took out a couple of his favourite home-made sticky syrup biscuits. A scrawled note on the back of an envelope was propped against the stained teapot. He picked it up as he stuffed a whole biscuit into his mouth. His gran had obviously scribbled it to herself, as a reminder.

'Be ready for Poppy. Picking me up 12-ish for Roughtor. Make pasties tomorrow. Meat in fridge. Post card to Ruth.'

Josh swore loudly. A mouthful of biscuit crumbs shot on to the table. The cat looked up, startled, from its dish of nibbles and jumped to the safety of a saggy armchair. The back door banged shut as Josh rushed out. Soon the jeep was making its way back on the road to Camelford. As he drove like a lunatic let loose, Josh talked to himself above the pounding beat of The Killers on the car stereo.

'What the hell is Poppy thinking of, taking Gran to Roughtor?'

He swore some more at the sight of a tractor chugging steadily along ahead of him. A red mist was rising in his eyes. Normally he had a lot of sympathy for tractors on the road; he knew from experience how difficult it could be, with impatient drivers behind, pushing you on and getting up your ass so-to-speak.

'They must be bleddy mad, the pair of them!'

He shouted and cursed as he overtook the tractor on a short stretch of straight road, low-chopped hedges on either side.

'Gran could have a fall. Anything could happen.'

But in the back of his mind he was more than just concerned, there was a creeping doubt that all was not well at Roughtor. Something more sinister than his gran having a fall was niggling in the back of his mind...

Poppy had lost all sense of time. She only knew that she was at Roughtor down by the stream and she dared not turn around. It seemed to be late afternoon now for the red ball of the sun was sinking in the west. On the bank, by the simple stone monument, Gweniver was talking to an unseen presence. Surely this was what Poppy had intended when she had brought the old woman to this special place? Now, after reciting the prayer in Cornish, Poppy felt calmer, more protected. Yet she still stood like a statue, afraid to move from the spot.

Gradually she had a sighting of a lone woman by the stone, wearing the same clothes Charlotte had worn on her last afternoon. She turned and Poppy could see the beads around her neck and the strings on her bonnet flying free. Her face was pale, like cold white marble for all its loveliness.

When she eventually spoke, she spoke in Gweniver's own low, husky voice.

'No, 'twas not Matthew Weeks who murdered me. He was forced into making a confession. They were all against him you see.'

Her beautiful face was indescribably sad. She

sighed, long and drawn out, and then looked up towards the craggy old face of Roughtor, frowning down on them.

'Another man waylaid me, after I left Matthee on the moor. We'd had bad words, you see, and in my foolish pride I struck off on my own, head held high.'

She wiped tears from her eyes with a green gauze handkerchief.

'The other man must have watched and waited until I was alone. He forced me down here to the riverside. At first I thought he was only fooling with me, I knew him you see. He was some years older than me, but I had been easily taken in by his handsome smiles and his pretty words and promises.'

Charlotte paused again, looking towards the sunset. As before, her beads took on the red light.

'I looked around me but there was no one to help me, not in this wild, lonely place. I realised then how foolish I had been. He tore my bonnet and shawl off savagely and kissed me so hard it hurt. He bit my lips and I tasted my own blood. I knew then this man would have his own way with me, so I turned my back on him, trying desperately to get away.'

She whispered, still in Gweniver's husky voice.

'He pulled my hair so painfully my head jerked back. My neck was naked but for my Sunday beads... and then he... then Tommy Prout sliced my throat across with a knife.'

Poppy's own blood seemed to stop pumping at the picture Charlotte had painted. She could only begin to imagine the terror of it all, those last moments of pain and knowing, as her blood gushed into the marshy ground and her coral beads lay broken and scattered. It was as she had thought. Tommy Prout had killed her, not Matthew Weeks. He had wanted Charlotte for himself, and could not believe it when she had fought and struggled against him at Roughtor ford. How easy it must have been then, to point the finger at Matthew. Tommy had hated him, everyone at Penhale Farm knew that. And how simple it was to get his uncle, Isaac Cory, to back his story up; for it was Cory who had later walked to the very spot where Charlotte's shawl and bonnet were buried in a marshy pit. It was Cory who was adamant that he had seen Matthew Weeks on the moor that Sunday evening from a distance of some three-quarters of a mile, to implicate him in her death.

In the courtroom, Cory had denied that he had ever quarrelled with Matthew Weeks over some lost bullocks. And his own nephew, Thomas Prout, was never even required to say where he was on that fateful evening. All these things raced crazily through Poppy's mind. Gweniver had voiced them, from the spirit of Charlotte Dymond herself.

The sun shone blood-red behind the granite pillar, causing a dark shadow to fall straight across the water. Again the husky voice, saying: 'I have haunted this place for many a year. I could never rest in peace you see, not 'til the truth be told.'

The vision of Charlotte seemed to smile then, before she slowly turned away. In the fading red light she gradually disappeared from sight and silence fell.

FORTY TWO

IN her head Poppy thought she could hear another voice, a man's voice, coming out of the dusk. Matt's voice. She felt she could look behind her at long last. Her feet were wet and cold from where she had been standing in the boggy ground below the stone. A shaft of light from the setting sun lit her tangled, long red hair, like a Rossetti painting. Pre-Raphaelite. And now Matt was calling her from across the stream. Poppy could not see him properly, the light from behind him was blinding. Why had he come to her? Hadn't she finally scattered his ashes? Laid him to rest? What was it that made him need to rise again, return to haunt the living? She thought she could see a hand beckoning her to cross the stream. His voice was calling her, telling her not to be afraid. Of course he would not leave her. She only had to cross over to be with him once more.

Visions of Matt, the Matt she had loved, came to her then out of the dusk. She saw his remarkable dark eyes, the beautiful crucifix silver at his throat. She imagined she could feel the touch of his olive skin, taste the sea-salt on his lips like that very first time. He was telling her how easy it was to be with him again, she only had to cross. She started to move very slowly towards the visionary light, as if in a dream.

The jeep skidded to an abrupt halt on the rough surface. Josh jumped out and ran towards the ford in the half-light. He could pick out a dark shape, bent over on a stone. It was his gran, Gweniver. Relief flooded through him but Josh soon realised she was as cold as death and totally exhausted. He even wondered if she'd had a stroke, for there was no recognition in her usually bright eyes. He wrapped her shawl tightly around her tiny frame and pulled off his own woollen sweater to give her an extra layer of warmth. All the time he was rubbing her cold hands and talking to her, reassuring her. If he didn't do something more for her, hypothermia would set in, if it hadn't already. He got out his mobile to phone for an ambulance and prayed there would be a signal despite being under the highest tors in Cornwall. The old Gods were with him.

But where then, on this darkening moor, was Poppy? He tried to get some sense from Gweniver, but there was only an inarticulate husky sound in response. He felt panic growing inside him, but he knew he must leave her to search for Poppy.

'I'll be straight back, Gran. You're a bit warmer now and the ambulance will be here soon. It's only down the road in Camelford. I've got to find Poppy... you understand, don't you?'

A barely perceptible nod from the shape that was Gweniver. Some sort of understanding then, he thought hopefully.

He turned towards the place where the stone monument stood in the dwindling rays of light, for surely he would find Poppy there. He shouted her name loudly and the only sound in return was the haunting call of a curlew somewhere out in the marshes and the trickling of water. Where the hell was she? He shouted again, his deep voice echoing over the soggy low-lying ground. Wisps of white mist were rising now, shrouding the black water.

A thin cry came from the darkness. Josh's instincts sharpened and he splashed through bog-water in the direction of the sound. He knew he must stay calm. A stumble in the marshes could be fatal.

'Poppy? Where the hell are you? Speak to me.'

His voice caught with emotion.

'Please let her answer,' he prayed, not for the first time that evening. The curlew's plaintive call was again the only response. Beams of light appeared from behind him, moving down towards the ford. The ambulance. What would they think of him, leaving a frail old woman, and his grandmother at that, alone in the darkness?

But he knew he must focus on finding Poppy now. His gran would soon be safe and looked after. In the beams of the headlights, he thought he glimpsed a slight movement and began in pursuit. She was standing still now, but she seemed to be speaking. Her untameable hair was wet with the clinging mist. Ahead of her, he was aware of the fast-moving water and the treacherous marshes.

'Poppy, stay where you are,' he shouted. 'I've come to take you back.'

He made his way carefully ever nearer her, feeling the ground underfoot. She seemed to be staring at something intently only a few feet away. Then she turned and seemed to rouse herself from her torpor as Josh stretched for her hand. She too was stone-cold, like Gweniver. Her hand felt like a child's in his own huge fist. He squeezed it tightly.

'It's going to be all right, you're safe now.'

Her pale face looked up at him.

'Matt is here for me, waiting for me.'

She looked at the spot she had been staring at before.

'He is getting angry with me now.'

Josh squeezed her hand once more and pulled her roughly towards him. He shook her.

'Matt is dead, Poppy. He is gone.'

Then he clutched her thin cold frame tightly against

his body for warmth. He whispered into her hair: 'Just like Charlotte Dymond is dead and gone too.'

Even in that moment he imagined he saw the white shadow of a woman lingering nearby.

'You know how I would do anything for you. But I will not allow you to destroy yourself in your search for the past.'

He took her hand and grasped it firmly.

'Come on, Poppy. You're coming back with me.'

It was dark now, only a streak of light shone across the surface of the black water, splintering into tiny stars.

She hesitated, then looked back over her shoulder into the darkness. A strong tug on her hand and she began to follow Josh. She turned away from the rank smell of marsh and the sound of trickling water, away from the ghostly granite stone wreathed in white mist. She knew then that her painful time of great loneliness was over. The ghosts of the past had disappeared. There was nothing to be afraid of.

As they made their way together through the darkness of the moor, she knew the spell was broken. She could face whatever the future held. Beside her there was such love and friendship. She felt strong. She could do anything.

They started to climb the slope from the ford through the soaking wet heather and dissolving mist, in the direction of the ambulance's spinning blue lights. Distant human voices carried comfortingly on the air.

High, high above them in the darkness, the eternal wind sighed and moaned around the ancient stones on the summit of Roughtor.

CHARLOTTE DYMOND

IN the spring of 1844 a young woman's body, with her throat savagely cut, was found in a lonely spot near the ford below Roughtor on Bodmin Moor. She was quickly identified as the missing milkmaid from Penhale Farm in the parish of Davidstow.

Charlotte Dymond was carried back across the moor on a hurdle to Penhale Farm, where she had been in service since an early age. And so began the tragic story of Charlotte Dymond, which has fascinated so many people down through the years and is still an enigma today.

Charlotte was born in Boscastle some 18 years before, the unwanted daughter of an unmarried schoolteacher. These were different times in North Cornwall and she was sent away by her mother and put in service as soon as possible, probably at the age of 11 years.

Charlotte, a pretty girl, worked as a domestic servant and helped with the milking. Penhale Farm was Charlotte's world back in 1844, under the watchful eye of Mrs Philippa Peter, a farmer's widow, who continued to work the land with her son John Peter and her servants, John Stevens and Matthew Weeks.

The work was hard, the hours were long, and there was little excitement. Weekends were a continuation of work on the farm and in the house, with the exception of the Sabbath when the whole household was expected to attend the chapel with the Mistress, at nearby Tremail.

Charlotte had been 'walking-out' with 22-year-old

Matthew Weeks for some time. He was an illiterate farm labourer from the parish of Lezant, near Launceston. He had a lame leg, which meant he walked with a limp.

Matthew made up for his lack of good looks with a set of fancy Sunday clothes. Charlotte is thought to have accepted Matthew as her young man for some time. He looked after her clothes in a box in the room he shared with John Peter and his fellow servant, John Stevens.

But something had changed in their relationship by April 1844, so that Matthew became morose and Charlotte more flirtatious with other young men in the neighbourhood.

On 14th April, Matthew and Charlotte walked out of Penhale Farm, up the lane together. Later Matthew returned alone, saying they had quarrelled on the moor and gone their separate ways. For over a week, Mrs Peter and, it seemed, the whole parish pestered Matthew about Charlotte's disappearance.

On the morning of 21st April, Matthew completed his chores and walked out of Penhale. Two days later, a search of the moor ended with the discovery of a young woman's body, near a stream below Roughtor. Charlotte Dymond had been found.

Constables started to follow the trail of Matthew Weeks. In the minds of most of the locals and even his workmates he was obviously guilty, condemned in his absence.

Matthew Weeks was arrested in Plymouth, the home of his sister. He was walking on the Hoe with her at the time of his arrest and did not want her to become distressed, as she was pregnant.

He was taken back to Hallworthy for a magistrate's hearing and from there moved to Bodmin Gaol, where he was charged with Charlotte's murder.

In August, after a one-sided trial, full of

inconsistencies, Matthew Weeks was condemned to death. He hanged at Bodmin Gaol on 12th August 1844. Many still believe he was an innocent man.

JANE NANCARROW

JANE Nancarrow was born in St Stephens, Launceston. She attended the old National School, where she was taught by the poet Charles Causley, whose *Ballad Of Charlotte Dymond* later fascinated and captured her imagination. She was a student of Launceston College and trained as a secondary teacher in Derby, where she played the role of Regan, Duchess of Cornwall in *King Lear*. She returned to Cornwall and taught English at Bodmin College for 30 years. She has written numerous short stories and performed with the North Cornwall and Camhayle Theatre companies in a variety of productions. She also appeared alongside Edward Woodward in the feature film, *A Congregation Of Ghosts.* Now a supply teacher, she is living back in St Stephens with husband Jim and son, Joshua. She also has a daughter, Polly, and a step-daughter, Naomi. Her short stories have been published in *Scryfa* and in 2008 she won the Gorsedd prize for a short story set in Cornwall. *Stones And Shadows* is her first novel.